NANCY STEWART

BEULAH LAND

A NOVEL

interlude  press • new york

"★★★★★... *Beulah Land* is a brave, refreshing novel that offers a message of hope... [It is] an accurate portrayal of what it's like to grow up in a place where your very existence is challenged, as well as a reminder that the willingness to push on wins the day, every time. *Beulah Land* is a much needed story of queer resistance and courage in the face of bigotry and intolerance."

—*Foreword Reviews*

"Nancy Stewart writes from the heart about a young woman of true grit in *Beulah Land*. Violette Sinclair, shaped by the culture of the Ozarks where she struggles to create her own selfhood, will not be limited by circumstance and definition by others. Stewart tells Violette's story with grace, vigor, and charm. Violette Sinclair wins through, and so does Nancy Stewart in creating this powerful tale of a young woman's personal 'favored land of Beulah.'"

—Gerald Duff, Author of *Playing Custer*
and *Nashville Burning*

"In *Beulah Land,* Nancy Stewart has crafted a winning combination—a fast-moving plot, and a fierce heroine worth rooting for!"

—Shannon Hitchcock, Author of *Ruby Lee & Me*

In memory of my cousin, Jill Rosenthal,
whose courage has illuminated the lives of so many.

In honor of Jill's life partner, Karen Fischer,
whose generosity of spirit inspires all who know her.

In tribute to my son, Colin August Stewart,
from whom I have learned the meaning of love.

AUTHOR'S NOTE

BEULAH LAND IS A STORY written from my heart to yours. The book's core is partly a family saga, although most of the novel came directly from my imagination. It is a narrative that I believe needed to be told for the greater good of women and, indeed, all people who strive for justice.

Even though, but certainly not because, Violette lives in a marginalized area of the United States, a profound message resonates within her story. It is one of determination, and courage, and hope. I hope readers of *Beulah Land* will take away certain basic truths: the reality of a timeless battle between good and evil, the strength of the human spirit and its ability to overcome unimaginable odds, and, most of all, the enduring fact that people everywhere are far more alike than different.

Violette Sinclair's dangerous journey in the Missouri Ozarks, particularly during her seventeenth summer, is unfortunately still a cautionary tale for many young people. Although gender equality has made substantial progress in the United States, the threat and reality of assault, including sexual assault, remains a clear and present danger to American women. While no one is raped in this novel, that act is threatened. In some scenes, a character is exposed to homophobic behavior, some violence, and unwanted touching.

This book has been read by two sensitivity readers and was approved by both.

Listed below are chapter references for trigger warnings:

Homophobia (Chapters 1-3, 17 and 33)
Violence (Chapter 9 and 33)
Potential violence (Chapter 11)
Result of animal cruelty (Chapter 13)
Animal cruelty (Chapter 32)

EDITOR'S NOTE

BEULAH LAND IS NOT AN easy read. It is not a romance, or an uplifting tale about a plucky teenager. It is, at times, difficult to read. So why would we, a publisher known for our commitment to stories with happy endings for LGBTQ characters, choose to publish this novel?

Two words: Violette Sinclair.

When I first read *Beulah Land*, I was moved to tears by Violette's determination. She is a force of nature, and we need more lesbian characters like her. I am proud to help bring this remarkable story to the world.

In this young adult novel, our heroine stands her ground in the face of bullies and bigots, protects her family and forgotten animals, and, despite her fears and the harsh realities of life in the Ozark mountains, charges forth to meet challenge after challenge. She is a bold, courageous girl who, through all of her trials, holds fast to who she is.

Violette is not a tragic LGBTQ character.

Violette *triumphs*.

Thank you for giving *Beulah Land* your time and attention.

—Annie Harper, Executive Editor

1

How can one decision lead to a lifetime of asking, *What if?* That question haunts me and it won't let go. But when Mama pushes our dilapidated kitchen window up, the noise makes my troubles evaporate like ghosts in a mountain mist.

"Hey, Mama," I yell. "Where's Jessie gone so early?"

"Violette! You scared the devil out of me. What're you doing sitting outside in the half-dark again?"

"Nothing. I'm coming on in." I stand up, careful not to smash my foot through that top porch step another time. Hundred-year-old floorboards creak when I reach the cluttered kitchen, and the reek of rancid frying grease makes my stomach lurch.

Mama swallows the last of her coffee, swishes the mug in soapy dishwater, and sets it on the scarred counter. "Well," she starts, like she's gonna give me the Eleventh Commandment, "Jessie went on over to the school to help Coach David with those freshman cheerleading tryouts, her being captain of the sophomore squad."

"Like I didn't know Jess is the captain, Mama."

She puts a squint on me. "I can't hardly keep up with that girl's schedule, she's so busy. You know, now she's got her a boyfriend. He's a good catch, being Pastor Akins's son and all."

"Yeah, Seth's an okay kid."

I lean close to the screen, suck in some sweet air, and wish I was already at work. But when I hear brakes squeal and see the burly guy with a buzz haircut and too-large hand-me-down jeans step out of his truck, Mama and my other worries are all but forgot. "Hey, Junior! Seeing your mug's already made my day. Get yourself on in here."

He ambles up to the window and gives me a grin. "Thought I'd stop on by, since my cell phone's outta juice. Can you go down to the lumberyard with me, or you gotta work? I told Daddy I'd build that extra chicken coop before school starts. Uh, we haven't had much time to talk lately."

"Sure, I'll be happy to go. It's Doc's late night, so I don't start till two."

Junior's got about the only air-conditioned vehicle I know of around these hills. I aim the side vent so cold air will hit my face and feel like a rich person when it does. "Real glad you came by, Junie." Anybody else calls him that, he'll make their face mashed potatoes.

"Yeah, me too. Like I said, it's been a while. Amberleigh, you know, she took up most of my spare time lately." He takes a breath to say more, then stops.

I peek over at him. Maybe he'll talk about their breakup. It hurt my feelings, because he never once said a word to me about any of it.

"Her daddy runs that big old meth lab up Morgan's Mountain," he says, like I didn't know.

"I heard about that place."

"Old Amberleigh, she wanted me to quit school and cook with her clan. Wasn't gonna happen, with me trying for a scholarship to Missouri State, so...I guess you'd say that was that."

"Well, Junie, nobody can cook meth and be a football coach, so you got it pretty right. If you ask me."

He gives me an agreeable glance. *Hmph.*

I fiddle with the air-conditioner vent again even though the cool air's hitting my face just fine. "Uh, you think senior year's gonna be any fun, Junie?"

"I ain't taking any bets on it."

"Yeah, but you fit in, being one of the football stars." I don't say, *Even if it is in a crummy nowhere place like Bucktown, Missouri.*

"Fitting in's overrated."

"Well, it ain't if you don't, Junior."

"Expect so. But you got a great job, Vi. Anybody in these whole hills would kill to be Doc's assistant. And I know you love it," he adds, like the cherry on top of a sundae.

I let it drop. Suppose when you're in, you're in. And a person can't see past that, even Junior.

He slows down once we turn onto Main Street so the winter-made potholes, deep enough to tear the guts out of a vehicle real good, won't damage his truck. Junior makes a wide turn, avoiding a humdinger of a hole, and swings into the lumberyard, biggest business in town. Folks gotta repair their half falling-down houses, especially when cold weather closes in. Ice storms are wicked in these mountains and can collapse a rotten roof faster than the devil dancin' on a barstool. Junior cuts his engine, and the cab fills up with air so hot I can't hardly stand it. "Want to come in with me, Vi?"

I shake my head. "Think I'll go to Price's for a Coke. Their air-conditioning usually works. Can we meet up over there?"

"Sure, but I could be a while with all the measuring and stuff."

"Don't matter," I say, half mad at myself for using *don't* instead of *doesn't*. "I got time this morning."

I wave back at him and wait for a beat-up John Deere combine to bump along Main Street. Picking my way across the neglected asphalt, I step up on the sidewalk and open the boot-scuffed door that has *Price's Bar and Grill* painted on it in used-to-be-white letters. The reek of a filthy grill and fried onions attacks my nose before I turn the knob. Only things on the menu are hamburgers, cheeseburgers, and fries, so you're outta luck if that's not what you want.

The dimly lit tavern's half full of stubble-faced Bucktown men home from working the quarry nightshift. They're knocking back beer and shots pretty good. A ton of cussing and wild laughter's going on until I get to the bar, then it gets quiet as the cemetery out on Old Marion Road.

"Well, lookee what the cat dragged in," a watery-eyed man with a purple-veined nose calls out. A row of eyes turns to stare at me.

What was I thinking coming in this place?

Another man, all pork and fried potatoes, with arms the size of whisky barrels and a head growing tattoos instead of hair, slides his super-sized butt off the barstool. He gives me a glare, then struts over to where I'm quaking in my flip-flops. I'm nose-to-nose with Dale Woodbine, the biggest bully in three counties.

He glances back at the bar. "Yep, boys, this one's queer enough to kill any good time. What you doing here, *Vio-lette*? Trying to join the rest of us guys?"

"Just… just getting a Coke. It's so hot."

"It's-so-hot," Dale mimics me in a singsong voice, then hawks deep in his throat and sends a gob of chewing tobacco too close to my arm. He wipes the dribble on his dirty T-shirt.

I raise my eyes to his slits and force them to stay there.

The skinny bartender waves a dingy bar towel at me. "You get on out of here, girlie, if you know what's good for you where old Dale's concerned."

"Uh, I'm going." I back toward the door and shiver like I see that haint Grandma talks about floating across folks' graves. Face on fire, I fumble behind me for the doorknob, turn it, and walk out.

Heat blazes off the sidewalk and dries my tears quick. Where the hell's Junior?

He's gotta be finished by now. Soon as I start across the street, he ambles out the lumberyard door. "Hey, Junior. Can you wait for a Coke? I don't want to go back into Price's."

"Sure, but why not?"

"Dale Woodbine called me queer and spit tobacco goop at me."

Junior narrows his eyes at the tavern. "Okay, that's it. Whole county's had enough of him, especially you. He's gonna apologize."

"No! He'll kill you. He'll kill anyone gets in his way. You know he's done it before. He'll do it again."

"That jerk is gonna get payback time, and I'd like to be the one does it."

"It's all right, Junior."

But it isn't. I'm pretty near collapsed inside. The heat's laying heavy on me, and I might be sick. "Thanks for…watching my back."

"No sweat. You been getting *my* back since we was six. C'mon. Let's get on outta here."

Something else has been laying heavy on me. Pressing me down too long. Now I need to tell Junie. "I never thanked you proper after… Brandy. You were the only one stood up for me, and I've been bothered by not saying anything all this time."

"Well, it was wrong what happened to you and her, way it was handled and all."

"I wish we'd moved like Brandy's folks did. They were the smart ones, scared enough to get out. But us Sinclairs would never leave." I'm sick to my soul at the truth of it.

Junior's brakes squeal when he pulls into Mama's spot in front of the house. "You were awful quiet on the ride home, Vi. Don't let that jerk get you down, hear? He ain't worth it."

I open the truck door. "Yeah. I'll forget about it at work today. See ya."

The echo of an empty house matches my mood. Plopping onto my bed, I rub my eyes until pins of white light appear. I concentrate on the worries deep inside me. I didn't have any before Daddy was killed. He used to call me special; said my eyes were clear blue as a September sky. But my daddy, *he* was the special one. Everybody says John Sinclair was the best Sunday school teacher this side of Beulah Land, the place it mentions in the old hymn about going to Heaven. Even for people like me. If Daddy hadn't been shot, things would be way different. Maybe Mama would care more about us. Well, me anyway.

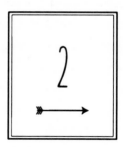

2

By the time I open the Hitchens County Animal Clinic door half an hour later, another summer thunderstorm is winding down. I fill my lungs with air, and a kind of contentment starts to take me over. Animals, and alcohol, and disinfectant, make a comfortable combination of smells; always calms me right down if I need calming. And today I need it.

Loretta, our receptionist, puts one of her hawk-eyed stares on me. "Hey, Violette. Have a bad morning? Y'all look kind of worried."

No, I'm fine," I lie. "What's up?"

"Well, sugar, we got us a busy afternoon. You have three cages to clean for starters, so you may as well get cracking. Oh, and would you fill the birdfeeders? New seed's here, and rain's pretty much quit."

"Okay, I'll tend to that now."

An inner office door opens, and a small dark-haired woman with the friendliest gray eyes walks out. I always think she looks too young to be a veterinarian. I study her white coat for the millionth time with the pocket that reads, *Claire Campbell, DVM.*

"Hey, Doc. I'm getting those feeders filled first thing."

"Terrific, Violette. I can always count on you, girl."

Mama should hear Doc call me *girl.* She'd think our Lord answered her prayers.

The storeroom's jammed mostly with lots of animal food, the kind that's better for your cat or dog than the stuff you buy at the IGA over in Blaylock. Problem is most folks around these parts can't hardly afford even the grocery store stuff. Most Ozarks animals live on table scraps and miss a meal or two more than I like to think about.

I flop a twenty-pound bag of birdseed off a middle shelf, cut a slit in the top, and tote it to the side door. A few raindrops splat on my head and arms as I step on the concrete pad, making me shiver.

A beat-up, faded red truck is parked partly on the sidewalk. Dog chow bags are loaded to overflowing in the bed. I squint my eyes and give what I'm staring at some thought. It's not Doc's delivery truck. Doesn't have the right kind of chow, either.

"Well, look who it ain't," a sarcastic voice says from the driver's side open window.

Dale! I tip the bag, and a birdseed mound piles up on the grass; least of my worries right now. "What... what do you want?"

"You got the question right, Sinclair, and here's the answer. I want you dead. You and that crazy witch maw of yours."

I suck in too much air and start coughing. "Why?"

"I got a old score to settle with your maw. Y'all go on and ask her. She knows what I'm chinwagging about, and she's had more'n a hunch this was coming at her, only a matter of time."

I remind myself to breathe.

"One other thing. You open your trap about this to like, say, the sheriff or any other law? Well, you got a pretty little sister who thinks guys is just fine. She'll get her turn to see how fine *I* am." He hawks up more tobacco juice, like it's his signature, and zaps it at me. Tipping the bill of his grubby baseball hat, he drawls, "You have a good day. That is, if you can, hear?"

I back up to the door and keep eyes tight on Dale. He's known to shoot folks for fun. *Where's my flip-flop?* Must have lost it in the wet grass. I shuffle into reception with one shoe on and my hair still dripping.

Loretta gapes at me. "I swan, girl. You're a sight. You get in a wrestling match with that birdseed bag?"

"Naw. Slipped on wet grass. Lost my shoe's all. I'll get it and clean up the seed pretty quick, but I want to dry out a little first."

"I THINK THAT TUMBLE DID you in earlier, Violette," Loretta tells me when I'm ready to leave for home this evening. "You sure spilling some birdseed's all that happened out in the side yard this afternoon?"

"Yeah," I say, too harsh-like. "Why?"

She gives me a hard stare over the tops of her granny glasses. "Girl, you been as jumpy as frog legs in a pan since you came back in here; like the devil himself is on your tail. Get some sleep tonight."

"Yeah, thanks, Loretta. See you tomorrow."

I hope with all my heart I will.

"THAT YOU, VIOLETTE?" JESSIE YELLS through the cracked-open front door. "I thought you'd *never* get home from work."

I shut the door tight, then slam the deadbolt home. "Well, it *was* my late night."

"What're you locking up for?" she says. "Afraid the bogeyman's gonna get you?"

"Never can tell. Where's Mama?"

"She's over at the church, helping with some kind of supper." Jess flounces her long, yellow hair then puts her hand on her hip. "You need to help me fix the zipper on my cheerleading outfit."

"I do?"

"Ye-ah. Mama said her eyes aren't good enough to see the place it keeps getting stuck, and the material's too cheap to change the zipper, and I can't afford a new outfit. You got nothing better going on now, anyway, do you?"

"A please would be nice."

Instead, I get a Jessie glare: She's like a cat sizing me up with those green eyes, all blackened around the rims. She flips her hair across one shoulder. "Well?"

"Go get it," I say, real flat.

I move a pile of raggedy old clothes Mama gathered up for the church missionary barrel to one side of the kitchen table and wait for Jessie.

"Here," she says, tossing the costume at me.

Spreading the flimsy costume out, I take a good look. "Should be easy," I mutter. "A two-minute stitch and glue job, and it's done."

"Yeah, sure," Jessie says, checking her phone.

"There. You have to let it set up now," I tell her. "Don't zip it until tomorrow, at the earliest."

She shrugs. "You always try to sound like that vet you work for. Putting on airs and giving instructions like a doctor or something."

"Jess, you know if I get to be a vet, I need to talk better, more like Doc Campbell. She grew up in the Ozarks way we did, and look how she talks now."

"Yeah, too citified to be from here."

I shrug. "Suppose it's from vet school in Minneapolis."

"Well, all's I know is putting on is gonna get you no place in these parts."

"You must be right. Uh, Jess, I need to tell you about something awful bad that happened today. Downright dangerous, in fact."

"Not now. I gotta give Jewel a call. Tell her my outfit's okay. Plus, you always got something awful to tell me. Nothing good. Ever."

Do I? I sit on our beat-up brown couch. "C'mon, Jess. Please. This is important."

She perches on the edge and frowns at me. "Hurry up, then."

"I DON'T BUY IT," MY sister says, after not interrupting for a change. "There's no way some strange guy would be after us. I mean, for what reason? I don't even know this Dale whatever his name is. You sure about this?"

"After listening to his rant? Yes, and that means you gotta be extra careful. I don't want to scare you crazy. But don't go places alone. You hear?"

Her gaze shifts away from my eyes, and she gives a tiny nod, but I'm not convinced she believes me or I believe her. "I have a suspicion there are secrets, Jessie, dark ones. And you and me? We're being dragged in because of Mama."

She picks up a plastic cat that Seth won for her at the county fair, examines it like it's a priceless treasure, and gently sets it back on the table. "So what can *we* do?"

"First, we gotta work out the real reason Dale's after us."

Jessie puts a smirky smile on me. "He's after *you* because you're not like us. Lots of folks around here's downright vicious about it."

I'm gonna ignore her ignorant attitude. "Don't think it's that simple anymore, Jess. I got a pretty big notion what's going on circles right back to Mama."

My sister sighs, gathers her hair in a hunk, and moves it to her other shoulder. "*If* what you're saying is true, Vi, we gotta go to the police."

"Won't do any good. I hear Sheriff Fletcher's real close to the Woodbines. Best friends and all. If *that's* true, nothing's going to touch Dale."

"Then we need to talk to Uncle Gray. With him being the clan head of us Sinclairs, it's his sworn duty to protect us."

"Not Uncle Gray. No. Not yet."

"Vi—"

"No! I can take care of this on my own."

"Why are you so stubborn if we're in this much danger, Violette? People in these parts get dead for a whole lot less than being gay. But since you are and everybody knows it, you got a real head start. You want that?"

"I don't. But Uncle Gray, he's got no respect or liking for me. Can't you understand *that*, Jessie?"

"Yeah, and dead's dead a long time. And you're saying *my* life's in danger now, so that's something *you* should understand." She flounces her hair back on both shoulders; a punctuation mark for being through with this conversation.

"I'm going out to get some air, Jess."

She doesn't answer, even when I slam the front porch door.

A lightning bolt zigzags between Bald Knob and Scoggins Ridge as I settle on the top porch step. Thunder growls like those Greek gods we studied battling over some old-timey feud. A few fat raindrops chill my thighs, and I brush them off.

Jess and Junior are pretty much right about me taking too many risks. I almost wish, for once, Mama would caution me on that. I long hard for her to love me for who I am. Mama, she always lays heavy on my heart.

WHEN I PULL INTO MY space behind Mama's car after work this afternoon, Aunt Zinnie's truck is here too. I slog across the soaked grass, happy the rain's stopped. The two of them are hunched on our front porch like a couple of ancient hags in a fairy tale.

"Well, hey, there, Aunt Zinnie and Mama. Y'all keeping your butts dry on those towels? Awful wet out here, you ask me."

My aunt's cigarette smoke swirls up like a specter in the mist. "Law, Violette, we're tough old birds; you ought to know that by now. Just came over for a chinwag with your mama."

Aunt Zinnie's not blood. She's married to Uncle Grayson Sinclair, Daddy's oldest brother. I like her: scrawny body all sinew and skin and her tongue sharp as a newly stropped razor. She's not mean, just sassy and direct.

"You holding your breath, waiting to say something until I maneuver these rotting steps, Aunt Zinnie? You sure got that look."

"You ain't far from the truth with those words. You made up your mind which way the wind's drifting, young'un, if you catch my meaning?"

Here it comes. I force myself not to glance at Mama, who's surely been chewing things over with Aunt Zinnie. Well, this is between me and my aunt.

She takes a long drag down to the filter of her cigarette then flings it onto the rocks next to the porch, where it glows red and then wastes away. Blowing smoke out her nose, she closes one eye and squints at me hard, but not mean. "It's like this, girl. Either you are or you ain't. Gay's what I'm talkin' about. Got a word of advice, though. You want to stay here in these hills there's rules ought not be broken, and there's consequences if they are. Law, child, I ain't telling you a thing you don't already know."

She stops talking and eyeballs all around, like we're sitting in a crowd of folks and she doesn't want them to hear. So, what on God's earth is she gonna say now? You never know with her.

"Your Uncle Gray, he agrees with me, girl. Lord, you don't want *him* on your case. You can bet he'll knock you upside the head sometime soon if you don't sort all this stuff out. I swan, Violette, it's already been four years since… that time. It's giving the whole clan a bad name."

"Aunt Zinnie—"

She shakes her finger at me. "Listen good, girl. With hurt and death put on your daddy, you don't want *that* to visit your door by having a uppity attitude about your affliction, if that's what you got. Be sensible's all I'm saying."

A chill hits me hard. "What… what do you mean about my daddy? Wasn't he killed in a hunting accident, like everybody says?"

"Not going there with you, Violette. Some things you need to jaw over with your mama, and that's one of them. You run on along now, while the two of us finish gabbing out here."

"But—"

"Y'all heard your aunt, Violette," Mama says.

"Okay."

Aunt Zinnie's got me so addled, I forget to mention that her tablecloth is in my truck, the one Mama mended and I didn't take back to her.

My breath catches in my throat when I walk into the shadowy kitchen. "Jessie, you half scared me out of my mind! What're you lurking in here for?"

"I listened out the window and heard what Aunt Zinnie just told you, and it's what everybody says, Violette. You gotta declare yourself one way or the other."

I peer out the screen window and lower my voice. "That right? Well, I expect you should pay no attention to whoever's doing the talking. And as far as *declaring myself*, it's nobody's business, including yours."

"Then you tell me how to pay no attention when it's *everyone* I know talking." Hands on her hips, my sister is fierce and furious.

"Why're you so mad? I don't go around flaunting my... sexuality. Just because of that one... incident in seventh grade."

"Well, that one *incident* was a doozy, wasn't it? In the girls' room with that Brandy, bare boobs smashed against each other, all kissy face? You call that nothing? I call it something, and so did the principal when she walked in and suspended y'all for three days. And now all our lives are... spoiled by what you done."

My insides churn when I think about doing that in school and getting caught. And Jessie's gonna keep talking about it.

She stomps closer to me. "And that's not everything. All you *do* is flaunt it! You got dyke wrote all over yourself. I mean, look at you. Baggy shorts or too-big jeans, and shapeless T-shirts are all you wear. And half the time no bra. Hell, any girl would kill for that figure and those legs—and your blue eyes with big old black lashes. Why're you like this? No matter what you do to yourself, you still look like a beautiful *girl*, Violette!"

She stops for a gulp of air, but I know there's more coming.

"And you got no girlfriends to talk about boys and stuff, like me and Jewel. You only run around with that Junior. I mean, he's got to be weird to run around with *you* of all people, him being the high school star linebacker. You never think what you do hurts me—or Mama, for that matter." Her bottom lip trembles, and her hands shake. She's done.

I'm wilted. Battered down and need to cry. "All I'm gonna say to defend myself is that you know how bad Mama beat me that time. I still have a couple scars. Probably carry them the rest of my life."

"Yeah, maybe they'll remind you how you screwed up *my* life."

"Tell me what I do, or think, or wear affects *you* in any way, Jess. Tell me." I hate myself for carrying this conversation on.

"If you don't know, I won't spell it out."

"Okay. Thanks for the heads-up." I turn and leave her alone in the kitchen. I bet the ugly look's still on her face.

When I stomp into the front room, Mama's in her recliner, family Bible propped on her lap. "Oh, did Aunt Zinnie leave?"

"What's wrong with you, Violette? Of course, she left. You got eyes to see I'm doing the Lord's work now. Let me get on with it."

"I would usually. But this can't wait. I wanted to talk to you earlier, but with Aunt Zinnie here…"

Mama takes her glasses off and glares at me.

"It's about that Woodbine guy. Dale. He… he keeps threatening me. He spit tobacco juice at me at Price's when I went to town with Junior."

I peek at her, and she has a funny glint in her eyes. "That all?"

"Isn't that enough?" I shake my head slow to make her wait for what's coming next. "Dale waylaid me outside Doc's this afternoon. Said he has an old score to settle with you, and that you know what he's talking about. And one more thing. If we go to the sheriff, he swore he'd hurt Jessie, and I know he would. Tell me what's going on. Is there a blood feud between us and the Woodbines?"

A frown and silence.

"Mama? I… I didn't want to, but I think we gotta go to the sheriff."

'No!" she shouts, so loud that I jump. "We won't go to any sheriff." She waves her hand real violent across her body. "No way. No how."

"But you know better than anyone around here how dangerous that clan is."

"What do you mean by that, girl?"

"N… nothing. Just you've lived here a long time's all."

She stares at me hard. "The Woodbines, they're strong-headed, is all. Willful, not dangerous. Why, I knew Dale since he was a young'un. Not a thing wrong with him that a good wife can't cure."

"And what about the threats against all three of us? What about Jessie? She's fifteen years old!"

"Don't you dare yell at me, Violette Sinclair, or I'll knock you upside the head. Worse, I'll have your Uncle Gray do it. Be a knock you surely won't forget."

"Oh, I see. You'll threaten me with a pounding from Uncle Gray but won't help your two daughters who're in danger from Dale Woodbine. That right? Is that right? Well, okay, then. *I'll* take care of Jessie and me. You care for yourself best you can."

I wheel on her from across the room. "You go on back and tend to the *Lord's* work now, and while you're at it, find a good wife for Dale. You know, one who can straighten him out before he beats her to death."

"What the hell's all this commotion?" Jessie hollers from our room. "I'm trying to talk to Jewel but I can't hear anything on account of the two of you yelling."

"Everything's okay," I lie.

Shaking all over, my head sort of echoes inside, but I'm joyful, and proud, and light of spirit. I've stood up to Mama for the first time in my life. But when I shift one last look back at her, a shiver snakes down my back. Instead of reading from the Bible or taking notes, she stares straight ahead, hardly blinking. Maybe she's in a trance, or had a stroke, or something.

"Mama, you okay?"

She says nothing.

I tread light to our room, like *I'm* the one in the wrong. "Jessie, I don't want to be in here any more than you want me to, but I gotta ask you something."

"What," she says, flat and mean.

"Uh, did you hear Aunt Zinnie talk about Daddy earlier?"

"No."

"She basically said his accident was really murder, and somebody got away with it."

Jessie stops picking at a mosquito bite scab. "What? Who'd do such a thing? Daddy never hurt anybody, did he?"

"Not that I know about, but like I said before, something's real messed up around here, more than usual, and we're gonna end up dead if we don't watch our backs. You and me, we need to stick together."

My sister's eyebrows knit into a frown. "Way I look at this so-called mess-up, Vi? You're the one with the problem, so if there's any danger, it's yours. Deal with it." She bounds off her bed and sashays out of the room.

I never knew my sister hated me so much.

4

A LITTLE SHIVER OF HAPPINESS runs through me when I pull into the clinic parking lot this morning and see Junior's truck. "Hey, what're you doing here?" I yell over Luke Bryan belting out "That's My Kind of Night." "Not that I'm not glad to see you or nothing... anything."

He leans over and flips off the radio. "Aw, I had to stop over at the lumberyard again. Knew you were working early, so... got any time off today? Need to talk to you is all."

"And I need to talk to you, Junie."

"About Dale?"

"How'd you guess? You too?"

"Hundred percent right, Vi."

"Can we talk now and still meet up for lunch?"

"Sure," he says, right as Doc drives up.

She puts her window down and calls, "Hey, you two. Beautiful day, huh?"

I smile at her. "Sure is, Doc."

Junior puts one of his brightest smiles on my boss. "Morning, Doc. Hope y'all have a fine day."

"Thanks, Junior. Same to you," she says.

"See you at The Shine-A-Mite, Vi." He pops the truck in gear and drives off.

Doc gives me a smile as sunny as the morning. "That's something nice to look forward to."

"Yes, it is." I wish she'd have shown up five minutes later.

I SLIDE ONTO THE COOL red vinyl seat across from Junior at The Shine-A-Mite, one of the only places in town where, if you're lucky, you may not come down with ptomaine. He picked the best booth; the one that has the least amount of stuffing poking through the seats.

"I ordered our usual burger and fries, Vi. Hope that's okay with you."

"That's great. I'm starved."

Junior wipes his sweaty face with a paper napkin that instantly falls apart. "At least the air conditioner's working now. A week ago it was broken, and they had to wait for a part from Springfield."

"Yeah, this heat's something else," I say. "You'd think it was middle of summer in Bucktown, Missouri."

"Always a smartass, Vi. That's why I love you."

"Glad somebody does, Junie. There's the truth of it."

The lunch crowd's milling around; never enough places to sit in this tiny place. Six overweight men dressed in overalls and not much else are squeezed into a booth made for two on a side. "Gotta stop eating squirrel and fried potatoes for supper, Luther, if I'm gonna eat lunch here on a regular basis."

"You're on to something there, Pervis," his booth buddy answers, digging into a hamburger dripping with ketchup and mustard.

The grizzled old guy behind Junior tells his just-as-shaggy friend, "My lettuce did squat this spring, but the rock crop? Gonna win grand prize at the fair in Sedalia."

I roll my eyes at that one. "So, what're you so bothered about you couldn't tell me this morning?"

He takes a long slurp of Coke and sets it back on the table in the same wet ring. "Well, I heard something sounds like trouble last night from a couple of Buzzard Ridge guys up at Bad Ass Bar." He rubs his stubbly chin and looks me in the eyes. "Word has it old Dale's got a bead from the business end of a rifle on you *and* your maw."

"Yeah, he was waiting outside the clinic yesterday. Threatened to kill me and Mama. Said if I told the law what he said to me, he'd hurt Jess."

"Why didn't you tell me?"

"I... uh... should have told you right away, but... I just didn't want to think about it anymore. What do you *really* know about Dale, anyway?"

"Pretty much same as everybody, Vi. He lives up top Hog Back Mountain in some kind of clan compound. They pay *no* attention to the law, like hunting out of season, poaching livestock, even killing folks who get in their way. You probably heard the toughest mountain men give that clan plenty of room."

"Yeah, I have."

He stares at me hard. "But Dale, he's something else. Word is he's killed a lot of folks around here, including old man Willis in a land dispute, and got away with it, mainly 'cause he's tight kin of the sheriff."

I stop unwrapping my straw. "Kin? I didn't know that. Thought they were just friends."

"Nope, cousins."

"Well, that sucks. I heard the mama's dead—just died, actually—and Dale's pretty broke up about it."

"Yeah, it's what I hear. But why would he want to hurt a crazy old lady like *your* maw? Uh, sorry, Vi."

"It's okay, Junie. I can't make out what's going on in her head, but like Jess and I talked about, she's carrying around dark secrets."

"Nobody's gonna care about any secrets your maw's keeping. She's not interesting enough. Uh, sorry again."

"But some people sort of follow her and think she's holy or something; like the healing finger she *says* she has." I wiggle my right index finger at Junior.

"Heck, Vi. Even around here, nobody's gonna believe that hogwash, unless…" He rubs his hair, stubble that would be the color of an acorn if he let it grow.

"What? What, Junior?"

"How about he brought in your mama to cure his maw, and it didn't work? That might be reason enough."

"Yeah, but Mama's always talked about being careful in giving your word around some mountain types. She says that the promise is everything, and you could end up dead if it's a lie. Or even if it falls through, and it isn't your fault. Wouldn't she take her own advice?"

He picks up his almost-empty Coke cup and shakes some ice into his mouth. "My daddy says the same thing, but to me it's just old-timey talk. I'd forget about that. Look, the way I see it, two things need to happen right away." He holds up his thumb. "First, you gotta go to the sheriff. I'll tag along if you want. Dale may be his kin, but Fletcher's the sheriff, and he has a job to do." His index finger goes up next to his thumb. "Second, you gotta find out about your mama's hang-up with the Woodbine clan. Why she's protecting them and all."

I nod but don't look directly at Junie. "Something weird's going on between Mama and those Woodbines. After the way she acted last night, I see it real clear; just don't know what *it* is."

"Well, you should find out. Dale, he's a maniac; no two ways about it."

"Thanks for offering to see the sheriff with me, but I need to go on my own. I don't want to drag you into this mess."

"I get that, Vi, but be careful with Sheriff Fletcher, you hear? He's one slippery dude."

"Sure thing."

By now he's made a design of water rings from his Coke cup pretty near all over his side of the table, and if I know Junior, that means he's still thinking hard.

"Thanks for caring about me, you hear? I appreciate it. I'm gonna try to see the sheriff this afternoon."

"Good, Vi. That's good. It's time for some action now that Dale's got y'all in his crosshairs."

"I'll let you know what I find out."

The middle-aged waitress with an ongoing cigarette cough slams two burgers and fries on our table. "Here's your usual order, young'uns. Hope y'all enjoy 'em. And I'll refill them Cokes for you too."

"Thanks, Cassie," I say. "I'm starved."

I'm just hoping a burger and fries aren't my last meal.

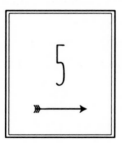

5

"SEE YOU TOMORROW. GOTTA RUN some errands," I tell Doc and Loretta at three o'clock, then thread my way through the people, dogs, and cats in the waiting room. My heart's kicking like a just-shorn sheep. Junie was right this morning about visiting that damn sheriff, but it's still scary to do.

The whole way over to the sheriff's office in Blaylock, I'm nervous as a June bug come the first of July. This town's the county seat and a heck of a lot bigger than Bucktown. Big difference I can see is stoplights. Bucktown's got none, so when folks visit, they don't know how to stop and go, never mind what to do with the yellow light.

I drive around the municipal building and park. A handwritten sign on the door says to go around front, and my stomach sinks to my toes. You never know who's driving by, and this whole county's nosier than Satan searching for sin.

I put my head down and walk around the building real fast, then tug open the heavy glass door. A lady with those half-glasses perched on her nose is at a wooden desk, beating her computer keys something ferocious. Her fingers in midair, she doesn't look at me. "What can I do for you?"

I fiddle with a couple of threads attached inside my jeans pocket. "I need to speak with Sheriff Fletcher, please." I'll be real polite first.

A shadow of a smile passes over her face. "You're in luck; he just walked in. What's your name?"

"Violette Sinclair."

"I'm sure he'll be happy to give you a minute of his time. What's this regarding?"

"Uh, it's private—if that's okay."

She stares at me, less friendly than before, but gets up, knocks on a door that says *Sheriff Boyd Fletcher*, and walks in.

I take time to eyeball the place. On a bulletin board behind the lady's desk is a tacked-up group of creepy-looking people with the title: *Missouri's Ten Most Wanted*. The creepiest is a guy with dead eyes named Rucker Hicks, wanted for arson and dogfighting. That may be something to tell Doc. Hearing a door open, I turn around, my body all quaky.

The secretary scoots out of his office, and the sheriff follows behind her. "Well, hello, young lady. What brings you for a visit?" Sheriff Fletcher, black hair slicked back, lean and rangy in his perfectly pressed tan uniform, is all smiles. When he offers to shake my hand, I see he's wearing a giant Bucktown High School ring.

I swallow too hard. "Would you mind if we went somewhere private, Sheriff?"

A flicker passes across his light blue eyes, then is gone. "How's about we talk in my office? That private enough for you?"

"Yes, sir."

He nods toward the door, and I'm amazed my legs hold me up.

The sheriff's desk is like the receptionist's, only bigger and a lot messier. The scent of cigars hangs heavy in the air, which is strange, because I'm pretty sure you can't smoke in a public building anymore.

Stepping around his desk, Sheriff Fletcher covers some papers with a yellow folder. If you ask me, there's nothing to hide. He's stalling, thinking about why I'm here, and I'm thinking he already knows why I'm here. "Have a seat and talk to me," he says, pointing to one of the heavy wooden chairs facing the desk.

I sit down sort of awkward-like and glance at my hands. They're rough from using so much water at work. My nails are broken, and there are dirt stains underneath that won't come out. I tuck them between the backs of my legs and the wooden seat. "I've come about Dale Woodbine."

Sheriff Fletcher drums his fingers lightly on his desk and sunlight from the window makes the huge red stone in his ring sparkle. "Meaning?" His voice is different, guarded.

"Meaning he's threatened to do me harm twice, and to kill me and my mama once, then said he'd… hurt my little sister if I spoke to you." The words tumble out too fast; my face is hot, and my body's all wobbly.

"Dale?" he asks, like he's surprised Dale would even say a cuss word. "Why would he do any of that to your family? Who *is* your family?"

A slight tic twitches above my right eye. "Sheriff, I'm being real respectful, but you know who my family is. The Sinclairs? We're born and bred in these parts for near two hundred years."

He glances away. "Oh, yes. I seem to remember the name. Well, Miss... Sinclair." He steeples his fingers on his desk the way I hate. "Problem is there's nothing I can do. You see, there has to be more than a threat. Otherwise, it's your word against his. Anyone hear him make these... so-called threats?"

"No, sir. He always does it when no one's around but me." The second I say those words, I know they're a mistake.

He opens the steeple and places his hands palms up on the desk.

"Well, then, like I stated, it's a he said, she said kind of thing, and, without evidence, your story won't fly." Pushing back his chair, he stands up and offers his hand again. I stand and shake it but don't want to. "Miss Sinclair, I thank you for stopping by and introducing yourself. Always glad to meet a fellow citizen. Sorry I couldn't be of more help."

He walks around his desk, then stops and puts a finger to his lips. "You know. About Dale. Sure, he's got himself into some mischief, time to time. But he's the kind of fellow who'd do anything for you. All you have to do is ask."

My breath catches in my throat, and I try hard not to cough. "Really?"

"And, uh, Miss Sinclair, at this time he's hurting bad because his mama just passed on. He was real close to her, being the baby and all. Why, after the doctors said there was nothing left to do, he even brought in some Ozark healers to help, but it was too late, or else they were no good. It'd be best if we all give him a little time."

Oh, my God! Was Mama one of them? Did she promise Dale to heal his mama and fail? I try to concentrate on the sheriff, but the conversation at Shine-A-Mite with Junior about broken promises has taken over my brain. I force myself to concentrate on Sheriff

Fletcher. "Thank you for listening to me. I'll be going now," I say in a voice as polite as peach pie. I'm not willing to burn *any* bridges, even with this lily-livered crook of a lawman.

STAMPING INTO THE HOUSE, I'M still steamed about talking with the sheriff this afternoon. I'm scared as hell too.

"Where you been?" Mama says in a snappish voice.

"Nowhere. Just a little late from work's all."

"That's not what I hear tell. Dewlene Jessop spotted you going in the sheriff's office in Blaylock. She called just to let me know." Mama puts the stink-eye real hard on me. "What you playing at, girl? Don't go lying, or you'll find yourself without a roof over your head."

I make my eyes all squinty and wonder in a vague way how Mama likes some of her own medicine. "You gave me no choice. When somebody threatens three members of a family, you have to do something. End of story." I leave her in the front room with her secrets and her Bible. I need to see my sister.

Jessie's sprawled all over her bed, talking so fast it could make you dizzy. Piles of her clothes are heaped on the floor even though she has her own chifforobe like I do. Stepping over them, I say, "Can we talk a minute?"

She clamps a hand hard over her phone and pitches me a filthy glance. "You got eyes to see I'm in the middle of an important conversation. You're just gonna have to wait until me and Jewel's done." Working her jaws, she blows a huge bubble, pops it like a pink punctuation mark, and goes back to the phone.

The front porch is always a lot friendlier than inside, so I wander out and sit on the top step, where the scent of rich soil greets my nose and calms me down. A soft breeze is blowing in from the west, and I'd give most anything to ride it to a place far away from here; maybe St. Louis, or Indianapolis, or Cincinnati, where somebody waits to love me and share my life.

Locusts are already singing on the evening air. The loneliest sound I've ever heard, they always remind me school's around the corner. One more year, and I'm out of here for good. Only thing I'll miss about this awful place is Junie's friendship; seeing him most every day and counting on him for the only kindness in my life.

After about fifteen minutes, Jessie wanders outside and sits down next to me. "Now, what the hell couldn't wait a bit of time."

"More threats of Dale Woodbine hurting you real bad, that's what."

It gets her attention.

Jessie has herself a steady bubble gum rhythm going, like her mouth's fixing to jump rope. She blows a champion-sized bubble, then sucks it in with a backwards swooshing sound. "Like I told you before, I don't buy any of this yarn you're putting to me. Dale— whoever he is—wouldn't go gunnin' after you on account of our Mama couldn't cure his mama. I agree with Junior on that one. Old-timey stuff's what it is, pure and simple. *And* your Sheriff Fletcher story doesn't make a *lick* of sense. He wouldn't stick his nose in something this... little. I mean, what's in it for him? You know good as I do that's not how he operates."

"Yeah, I thought of that, too. But what if Dale and the sheriff are in cahoots about something to do with us, and they stick together for that reason?"

Jess picks a sliver of popped bubble gum off her lip. "Maybe. Only maybe."

"Well, what he really said was for me not to go to the law or he'd...you know."

"Okay, so you and Dale got... gay issues, Vi. And where Mama's concerned, it could be about anything, living here her whole life; you know, pissing off people. She can do that real good. Well, I'm not gay. I love guys."

"Yeah, too much."

"Oh, get real. You know what I mean."

But she actually gives me a big old smile, and I consider it a gift.

A LUMPY PATCHWORK QUILT IS all I can see across our room in the dim morning light. "You still asleep, Jess?"

The quilt changes shape while she stretches. "Nope; just waking up."

"Got any plans for today?"

Jessie yawns so big, I hear her throat catch. "Not much with cheerleading tryouts done."

"Then would you mind driving up Hog Back with me?"

"Vi—"

"No, listen. I gotta visit that Woodbine Compound Junior told me about yesterday; see if anything's there that could help us out. Look, we'll be extra careful, but I figure it's always good to have as much information as possible on a person who's trying to murder you."

Silence from the lump, then a big sigh. "I got a bad feeling about this, but you surely can't go alone, so. . ."

"Thanks, Jess!" I say before she changes her mind. "You take your huge dark glasses, and I'll get that ratty headscarf of Mama's, so we'll have a little disguise. Let's leave nice and early, before the sun starts scorching everything."

"Okay," she says. "And before Mama gets all nosy about where we're going."

I can tell Jess is warming to the idea. A little, anyway.

THE ROAD'S BUMPY, THE BUGS are fierce, and the sun's too hot for this early of an August morning.

I glance over at Jess, who's sitting like a stone statue. "Like I said, we'll be real careful up Hog Back. The doors are locked, and we won't get out for anything."

"Okay, Vi."

She doesn't sound convinced.

Once we reach the mountaintop, I follow the sign to Cooter's Crick and then turn left onto a ruined ribbon of asphalt meant to be a two-lane road. We rumble by ramshackle barns, falling down fences, and old farm equipment left where it died, rusting away. I swipe at sweat covering my top lip. "How does mail get delivered around here? Even if you had an address, the mail-boxes don't, and these cabins are tucked away like Easter eggs in a cornfield."

"Heck if I know, Vi, but I'm scared, us squeezing down to a dirt one-track trail like this one."

"Yeah, I don't much like it, either. Two cars could maybe inch by, but they'd have to work real neighborly to do it."

Eww. Jessie jumps back and then ducks as a super-sized insect buzzes through the front windows, then is gone. "All these bugs are creeping me out. Gross."

"At least they're not ticks. Gotta find a turnaround. You see that row of beat-up mailboxes ahead on my right? Let's go over there, see if they got any names."

My tires crunch soft on the gravel as the truck rolls up to the boxes. Jess whispers, "Woodbine. On all five of them."

Funny how you can stop breathing, but your heart kicks up to jet-propelled. I point to where the branches of a young maple tree begin. "Look at the sign nailed up there. Not too friendly."

"Oh, I don't know. I think it's sociable far as skull and crossbones go," Jessie says, real sarcastic.

"Well, it's homey all right, if you like a jagged handsaw look. Your call, Jess. What should we do?"

"How about we drive a little way down there? Don't appear anybody's around."

I put the truck in gear and move forward. The track leads down a slight hill. The bottom is sort of carved out from zillions of gully-washers, and muddy water's standing in it from the storm two nights ago. Dragonflies skim the surface, leaving the tiniest of ripples.

"Better drive through that stuff slow as you can, Vi."

"Yeah, I will. Hey, Jess, look to your right. One of those root cellar's been carved into that limestone. Probably been there a hundred years or more, by the looks of the decrepit door and all."

"Wow, I don't even see a house yet. How'd Mama like going back and forth to *that* place for her put-up vegetables?"

"I snort. "It'd be too far, even for her.""

Jess points down the dirt driveway. "Wait. I see two cabins almost on top of that rise. Pretty rough, you ask me."

"Other three have to be around somewhere." A hound dog on a long chain raises its head. "Please don't start barking. Be real welcoming now." The gray-muzzled dog takes a sniff or two, then lowers its head back to the ground.

Thud. A door slams, then a motor revs up behind us. A deep voice with the accent of somebody mountain-born and -bred booms, "Halt! Halt! I'll shoot."

"Where'd he come from?" Jessie whispers.

"Don't know, but I can't outrun this guy. He'll shoot the tires flat. Not a word, you hear? We're gonna be fine," I lie. A filthy, rusted-out blue truck slams up behind us with a windshield so dirty, I can't see anything through my rearview mirror.

Jessie squints back. "I think he's aiming a shotgun at our heads through his front window. Here he comes."

The truck roars around us and lurches to a stop at my door. An old man with a tobacco-stained beard and a mouth holding no teeth, far as I can tell, points a shotgun directly at my head. "You're trespassing, girlie. Cain't you read?"

"Yes, sir," I drawl, trying to act tough like him. "I saw the sign, but everything looked so peaceful and the land's so pretty, I wanted to take a look-see's all. Sorry if I done wrong." I force my eyes to stay with his; I'm telling nothing but the gospel.

He stares a long spell through cold blue eyes that I'd wager have no heart behind them, but he breaks eye contact first. "Who're y'all? What parts you come from?"

I lift my chin real brave, but my body trembles. "Ross. Vi Ross. My family's Ozark bred for a coon's age. This here's my little sister. You must heard tell of us?" I'm praying he buys what I'm saying. It's mostly true, anyway, with my middle name being Ross,

Mama's maiden name. Please God, keep him from asking who my daddy is.

The man scowls at me but partly lowers his gun. "I know the Rosses, but that bull story of yours don't explain what in tarnation you're doing up here on my land."

"Sir, I... I don't know what else to say. I'm sorry, like I mentioned. Won't happen again."

"Better not, 'cause if it does, y'all's goin' home in a flour sack. That there's a solemn promise from Walter Woodbine."

I shudder right through the August heat. This guy's Dale's daddy, husband of the dead woman. "Thank you, sir. You got my word it won't happen again. Can we go now?"

"Y'all get on outta here before my boys come back. Be hell to pay if they find you up here. You just lucky you ran into me first, girlie." He spits tobacco juice on my truck's door, and it runs down the metal, leaving a foul smell. "I'm the nice one."

I nod at him, then turn the truck around toward the road. I'm trembling so hard I can hardly hold the wheel; my back tingles, expecting a slug to slam into it; and my legs are jerking like a pithed frog.

"That was close," Jessie says, her voice quaking.

"Too close. I must be outta my mind putting you in this danger, Jess. I'm sorry, so sorry."

"Way I look at it is, we survived, and now we got a story to tell someday, when the time's right."

I give her a thin smile. "If there's any good come out of this... meet-up, it's I finally see firsthand how dangerous these Woodbines are. Not to be trifled with, like Grandma says about people like them. Well, Violette Ross Sinclair has done her last trifling on this mountain."

"Maybe you're gonna start making some sensible choices about danger."

"Surely hope so," I say.

But I may not have that kind of choice to make.

"VI? VI, YOU AWAKE?"

"Just barely. It's not even six o'clock yet. You paying me back from our mountaintop adventure yesterday?"

"No, I wanted to talk to you about something then, but there never was a good time with that Woodbine guy and all." Jessie's wide-awake voice tells me she hasn't been asleep for a while. "I... I really need to talk to you."

A surge of danger blasts through me like a round from Mr. Woodbine's shotgun, and I sit up. "What's going on?"

"I... I don't feel so good, like I'm sick or something."

Lying back down, I want to throttle my sister. "That's all? You scared the living daylights out of me. I thought it was something about those damned Woodbines."

"No, nothing like that. Can I come over and sit on your bed?"

"You don't have to ask me."

Jessie's bed creaks when she gets up, and mine does as she sits down. She lowers her head and rubs her hands together like you see some old people do. "I think I'm pregnant. Almost sure of it."

The clock in the front room chimes, and I count the strikes. Six o'clock. Mama will be getting ready for the garden. My mind goes blank. *What do I say?* "Jess, are you sure? You've said lots of times your periods are... not right."

I force myself to look over at her and can just make out the shine of tear tracks down her cheeks.

"I know, but I've missed two, and I feel funny. Weird. Kind of sick on my stomach, and I'm so tired. What else could it be? I'm real scared, Vi, mostly of Mama. Plus, I'm too young to have a baby. I'm a kid myself. I wouldn't know what to do with one."

"I'm not gonna lay any guilt about being too young to get pregnant. That won't help anything."

"Thanks," she says, in the tiniest voice. "Thing is, I can't even buy a test. Only place in town to get one's Discount Dollar, and lots of my friends or their mamas work there. It'd be all over the Ozarks in a blink."

"Well, you're right about that. Everybody in the county shops there. Personally, I don't get the attraction. Lots of the stuff looks like it's already used before you bring it home." I put out my hand. "But here's the important thing. Have you told anyone yet? *Anyone.* Seth? Jewel? Be honest with me."

She shakes her head. Hard. "No! No one. I swear. If this gets back to Mama, she'll throw me out of the house. I know her. She will."

"I'm afraid there's truth in that, Jess. We'll have to drive over toward Branson and hope we don't lay eyes on anyone we know."

"I shouldn't a let this happen. Seth, he had protection. Most of the time, anyway. But it wasn't enough, I guess."

I let that one go.

She hesitates, then glances at me.

"Vi, saying I'm sorry now for the way I treated you with… what I just said about my… problem. It's a bad time 'cause it seems so… phony. But you gotta know how I feel. I've been real harsh on you. Said things about you—and to you—won't happen again. *Ever.*" She wipes her eyes and sniffs hard from down her throat.

Her apology sits hard on me. I want to believe her words, but that's gonna take time. How much, I don't know. "We'll chew this stuff over later, Jess. Don't fret about it now. I'm off work today, so you and me, we'll go on over toward Branson to find a Walgreens or CVS."

"Vi, I—" She pushes her feet into a pair of flip-flops and shuffles into the bathroom.

A soft breeze wafts through the screened window, along with a murky light signaling another dawn. I shiver under my thin T-shirt. Who knows what misery this day might bring? A young girl unprepared to have a baby? A family so stressed out by each other that a young'un could tip it right over? "Lord have mercy," I whisper, surprised and then ashamed that I sound exactly like our mama.

I SWALLOW THE LAST DROPS of coffee from my thick brown mug, swirl it in the remaining dishwater, and turn it upside-down to drain on a timeworn kitchen towel. "I left Mama a beat around the bush note, Jess. It's better not to outright lie to her. Now let's get out of here before she comes back in from the garden."

Jessie nods and heads for the front room. When she looks back to see if I'm coming, her pinched face and set mouth practically break my heart. *I reckon sisters are sisters, no matter what happens between them.* I remind myself to recall this moment when words and times get ugly between us again.

Once outside, we trot across the front yard, slide onto the truck seats, and shut the doors quiet as possible. Jessie's fingertips drum a nervous beat on her oversized pink plastic purse. "God, I'm already hot and sticky. How far do you think we'll have to drive to get to a decent-sized store?"

"I figure about thirty miles. Hey, Jess? Want to get lunch afterwards at Applebee's? You love their fries, and it's my treat."

"Sure. That'd be great."

I reach across and squeeze her hand. "Good. We have to eat somewhere, no matter what."

"You're worrying about this test too, ain't you, Violette?"

"A little. You're my sister, and I care about what happens to you."

"Vi… I know."

We ride in almost silence for about half an hour, which is unheard of for Jessie. I point to a highway sign that tells us the town of Layton is two miles ahead. "Okay, let's stop here," I say. "I know you don't care about it now, but this little town all cozied up to the Ozark foothills way it is? Real cute to walk around and stuff."

"Yeah," she says, like she didn't take in what I said. Can't blame her.

"Anyway, Layton has a little mall, a Sears and Penneys, and some shoe stores, stuff like that. Way better than Discount Dollar. And way safer for our needs."

Soon as we turn onto the off-ramp, she points out her window. "I see a Walgreens; might as well get this over with."

I park the truck by the front door, right next to the empty handicapped space. We look at each other and try to smile. Jessie gets out of the truck first, and I follow her inside. Automatic doors swish open, letting chilled air and about a million aromas assault my nose, with perfume winning the battle. "Looks like Family Planning's at the back."

She gives me kind of an unsteady nod. "I'm gonna get two pregnancy tests, different brands, Vi. I'll give you the money, but will you pay?"

"Sure."

"Back in a minute."

I stand at the front of the store and stare at two cashiers staring at me. Looks like they got nothing to do either. Turning around, I pretend to study a rack of suntan lotions, something I sure never use. Only folks that use this stuff are tourists, like over in Branson laying around by their fancy hotel swimming pools.

"Here you go, Vi," a weary Jessie voice says from behind me. "I'll wait somewhere close by."

She hands me the two packages. I make sure not to glance at them and hope the cashiers don't think they're mine. A pang of guilt zaps through me, and I try to shake it off. *Come on, Vi. She's just asking you to pay for them. Be a good sister.*

I take my time strolling over to the closest cashier, a middle-aged woman with hair dyed the color of coal. "That all today?"

She doesn't look at me, and I wonder why. No interest, or is she embarrassed at what I'm buying? I shake my head. *Get a grip, Violette. Nobody around here cares what the hell you buy.*

I try to smile. "Yes, thank you."

She rings up my purchase and drops it in a plastic bag. I give her the money; she hands me the bag. "Have a nice day."

I find Jessie trying to look inconspicuous, pretending to choose paper napkins from a bin. She makes a face at me when I hand her the bag. "Here goes."

"I'll walk over with you and wait right outside. Call me if you need anything."

"Yeah. Okay." We don't say another word as we trudge down the longest hallway in the world.

Jessie stops at the ladies' room door, turns to me, and says, "I'm going in now."

Her face is empty of color; her eyes are two wells brimming over with worry. My heart hurts for her.

When the door closes, the image of a steel trap with giant jaws fills my mind, and I try to make it go away. I wait a long time, too long. Then the toilet flushes. Looking to see if anyone's coming, I put my ear against the door. Nothing. At least no crying. That could be a good sign, or maybe not. Paper's being pulled out of a dispenser, then silence. Should I call to her? No, wait another minute.

When the door finally unlocks, I jump. Jess opens it and stares at me like those deer you see in your headlights at night.

I don't blink. "Well?"

My sister scrunches up her face and starts to sob.

I wrap my arms around her. "Jess, Jess, it's okay. We'll get through this together. It happens to lots of girls."

"No. It *is* okay. I'm not pregnant. Vi, I'm not pregnant. Don't know why I missed those periods, unless it was that bad flu I had a couple months ago, but everything's okay."

Jessie lowers her head on my shoulder and starts crying again, as a clerk walks by the door. "Everything all right, ladies? Anything I can do?"

I shake my head. "No, thank you. My sister, she's just… happy."

"Glad somebody is," he says and trudges on down the hall.

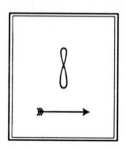

"No more sex," Jessie says, maneuvering an Applebee's ketchup-covered fry into her mouth.

"You say that now, but if you stay in a relationship with Seth or anyone, you should think about the pill."

"Yeah, I know, but after this scare, I'm not getting near a guy." Jessie pushes the salt and pepper shakers around the table. Something else is hard on her mind. "Vi, I don't want it to matter that you're gay. I'm not understanding it or something." She shakes her head. "I ain't saying this right. I mean, the way I lit into you about how you dress and all the other day, I acted bad and was ashamed of myself the second I said it."

I shift my weight on the booth's green plastic seat. "Look, Jess—"

She keeps on talking like she didn't hear that I interrupted her. "I know I kind of…apologized this morning, but please, please believe how *much* I mean it. I'm so tired of gay bashers, and… I'm tired of being one. I need you to help me."

When I put my hand on her arm, she doesn't yank it away or rub the place I touched like she'll get leprosy. Instead, she puts her hand on mine and says, "I'm gonna try real hard to be… a good sister."

I own the world, this second.

"Uh oh, looks like she's on the warpath," Jessie says, as I park the truck behind Mama's car a couple hours later.

"Yep. Thought she might be." Mama reminds me of one of those department store mannequins, the way she's leaning against the front porch next to the spent forget-me-nots she loves so much.

She's giving us the serious stink-eye," Jessie whispers.

Mama traipses over to the truck. "Where you two been? That so-called note told me exactly nothing. I tried over and over to call you, and nobody picked up. What if I needed something or had an emergency? What then?"

Jessie shuts her window, opens the door, and climbs out. "We decided quick-like to drive to Branson, Mama, with Vi having the day off and all. Nothing troubling about that, is there?"

"Surely is if you're lying to me."

I gotta tell Jess not to ask Mama that kind of question. It gives her too much power. Opening my door, I walk around the truck. "Well, we're back to help out, if you want."

"Help out, nothing." Mama's foot's a jackhammer at full speed. "Deputy dropped by here after y'all left. He was carrying a paper, all legal-like. It's against *you*, Violette. Calls you the defen-dant."

A tiny lick of fear touches my spine. I look down, not wanting Mama to pick up any of my fright. "Well, let me see it."

She whips a scary-looking envelope out of her apron pocket and hands it to me. Mama's far too anxious to deliver bad news. And by the look of the ripped flap, news she's already read. I force my hand not to shake when I take it from her.

Jessie walks over to me. "What's it say? You haven't done wrong."

The envelope is heavier than I expected. "I need to sit down and concentrate on this, Jess."

Mama thumps the document with her soil-stained finger and almost knocks it out of my hand. "Says here it's a restraining order to stay off Woodbine property, and you was there under false pretenses by using a fictitious name. If you turn to the last page, you'll see who signed it."

I try to study the paper but nothing makes sense to me yet. "Well, looks like three folks. Walter Woodbine, Sheriff Fletcher, and some judge named Sallee."

"Judge Sallee's not just *some judge*, Violette. He's real important. Why, he's kin to Walter too. You're lucky not to be in jail, snooping around up there."

"What I am doing, Mama, is trying to save our lives. If you'd cooperate and tell me what you know about those Woodbines, maybe we could clear this situation up."

"I don't know a thing about them. You better pay some mind to that summons, or whatever it is, or you're gonna land in jail," she tells me. For a second time.

I don't answer her and walk in the house, legal papers fluttering in my shaky hand.

Jessie pads into our room after me. "What're you fixing to do about that?"

"I need to read it better, but it looks like I gotta send it back to the courthouse with my signature, then stay away from the Woodbine property. I thought they had to give stuff like this to you in person, not to your mama. You always see that on TV."

Jess shrugs and picks up the paper. "Could be in these parts they don't follow the laws so close. That's my thinking, anyway."

"Yeah. Maybe signing this'll be the end of Dale's threats. I mean, he got the last word."

Jessie looks at me like she wants to believe it but doesn't, and truth be told, my words sound hollow to me too.

*   *   *

FIRST THING ON MY MIND this morning is that summons. Shivers of fear travel up and down my spine every time I think of it. And I can't get it off my mind, even at the clinic. Between being afraid and feeling like a criminal, this might be the longest day of my life. Why did I go up Hog Back and take Jess with me? It was stupid. And selfish. Not sure I'll ever grow up proper and be like Doc, a real adult.

The only good thing about today is Junie's stopping by after work; maybe take a drive. I need to talk to him. Seems like it takes a century for five o'clock to roll around. But when it does, I pick up my briefcase, the one that looks just like Doc's. It's the same weight as always, but today I'd swear I'm lugging every legal paper in the world.

Doc walks out of her office and studies me. "You look tired, Vi. Something worrying you?"

"No, not really," I lie. "Nothing that can't be fixed, anyway. Uh, see you tomorrow."

The look she put on me lasts a little too long for my way of thinking. "Have a good evening and get some rest."

"Sure. I'll try, Doc."

I lay my phone on Loretta's desk. "I'm supposed to meet up with Junior in a few minutes."

Doc gives me a smile. "I think you mean now. Look who's here."

The front door swings wide open, and Junior strides in. "Hey, Doc. Loretta."

He winks at me. "Ready to go?"

"Yep."

"See you," Junie and I say at the same time.

"You two take care—but have fun," Loretta calls.

Junior opens the door. "I got your text, Vi. What's up?"

"How about let's take a drive? Missed seeing your smile. I'll park my truck at Shine. Happy to help pay for gas, if you need some."

"Great. Good idea. Not the gas, though. I stopped by Rocket on my way over here and filled it up. Door's unlocked," he says, sliding in the driver's seat. He flips on the AC. "Hot as hell in here."

"Before we take off, Junie, I want to show you something. I got this restraining order after driving up Hog Back the other day with Jess." I pull my copy out of my case. "Can't go on Woodbine property anymore."

"Now what you got yourself into? Why'd you go on their land in the first place?" He takes a long look at the document, shakes his head, and hands it back. "You ought not to have gone up there, Vi. You take too many chances, with the way some people around here feel…"

I interrupt and start talking fast. "This is from Judge Sallee. You ever hear tell of him?"

"Yeah, my brother tangled with him over some meth charges. Daddy, he knows Sallee pretty good, him being our blood somewhere down the line. He went easy on Jake; first time offense and all."

"How's he doing not cooking?" I gotta get the topic off me even though I started it.

"Damned if I can figure it. He's not working but has plenty of spending money. I don't ask questions anymore, but I'm afraid for him."

"That old meth gets in your blood even if you don't use it personally. Money's too good, I figure. Doesn't appeal to me, Junie."

He gives a little chuckle, but it's got no happiness in it. "Me neither. Ain't worth being blown up in the cooking or spending a hunk of your life over at the big house in Jefferson City."

Junior shifts the truck. "I got an idea. You forget about Dale and that summons, and I'll forget about Jake. Let's take a longer ride and eat supper out. My treat. Okay?"

"Sounds real good."

"How about we take the old roads up Bald Knob?"

"Fine by me, Junie. Anywhere with you is fine with me."

"Vi, I…"

I look over and Junior's blushing like he's got a bad sunburn. "What?"

"Nothing. Nothing at all. Hot in here, even with the AC. Want to open the windows goin' up the mountain?"

"Sure." When I lower mine, cooler air rushes in along with the sweet smell of pine. "I'm happy, Junie. It always amazes me how beautiful this place is, the hills and valleys. Even the shabby little towns look nice at a distance."

"Hey, how about eating at that little roadhouse other side of Sinclair Mountain? That okay with you? I mean, some of your kin could be there, this close to the mountain."

"Junie, I'm so contented right now that Uncle Gray could walk in, and I wouldn't be jumpy."

Junior thumps the steering wheel with his thumbs and glances over at me. "I know Gray Sinclair's a feared man round about here. But why? He's not a killer like Dale, but he's got a fierce reputation. You know, folks dare not cross him."

"That's the right word; fierce, I mean. Even Aunt Zinnie, stroppy as she is, gives him lots of room. He runs the Sinclair clan like a general; no one better get out of line, or hurt any kin, or not pay their debts, or they'll answer to him."

"But with you that time, Vi. At school, I mean. He didn't do squat to protect or... avenge you, I guess is the word. I never could figure that one out."

"I... I don't think he knew what to do. I mean, there probably wasn't anybody in the whole Sinclair clan like me. Uncle Gray, he treated me real cold; still does. It used to hurt my feelings, but now... Guess I'm used to some folks not being so nice to me, and he's one of them." When I glance at Junior, he's got an odd look in his eyes. Maybe he's trying to figure out my crazy clan. *Good luck on that one, Junie. Ain't no use in even trying.*

I puff out a breath of air at a remembrance. "You know, my daddy always said Grayson Sinclair was the handsomest man in these hills, but to be honest, with a permanent frown carved on his face, I surely can't see it."

"He's got a power to him, though, Vi. Makes folks watch him and listen."

"Well, I'm so satisfied this evening, he could stroll right on in the restaurant and I'd give him a big old smile and say I was pleased to see him."

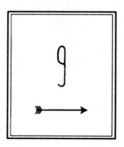

9

Darkness has nuzzled the hills by the time Junie and me pull around back into The Shine-A-Mite parking lot. "Looks like my truck's been okay sitting here. I had a great time. Thanks again for supper and our talk. I... I appreciate your friendship. Don't tell you enough."

"It's okay," Junior mumbles in his growly voice, the one he uses when he's embarrassed.

"Junie? I... I wish..."

"I know, Vi. Me too."

We sit and stare at each other a second. My heart's pretty near to breaking with what could have been. But there's nothing else to say, life being what it is, like Daddy always reminded me.

I unlock my door and wave; code for *Go ahead. I'm fine.* His truck lurches into gear; its taillights brighten as he waits for a car to pass. Turning left, he disappears down the road, leaving me with a hollow place carved out in my middle.

Scrambling into the truck, I elbow-lock the door. My engine purrs when I give it a touch of gas, but backing out of the space, something's not right. It's like none of the tires will work. A flash of fear lights my body up. Feels like somebody slashed 'em. Now what?

I'm scared to get out and scared to stay in. My phone. I grope around the seat for it, then rummage around in my briefcase. Damn! It's on the counter by the *Vaccinate Your Pet* fliers. Put it down telling Loretta goodbye. *Okay. Get into Shine. Fast.*

I scarce clear my door when something tears into me, and I'm flung to the ground like that birdseed sack on the soaking grass. My left cheek and elbow are on fire, and my brain's all lit like the Fourth of July. Can't get up; a boot mashes my chest. A shadow covers me like a funeral shroud. My mouth doesn't want to work. "What-you-want?"

"One answer, Sinclair. What're you farting around my property for?"

"Nothing."

"Yeah? Ain't the way my pappy sees it. He said you was snooping, looking around for something. What." *Bam!* "Was." *Bam!* "It?" *Bam!*

My head. Asphalt-slammed.

"Gross! Don't puke on me."

Jackboot. Face is raining red.

"C'mon, Dale." A voice floats in the air. "You all but killed her. She got the message. You can take that to the bank."

"Shut your gob, Rucker. I'm done when I'm done, and I ain't done."

Thud! White brain light. *Sweet Jesus, I'm dying.*

"Now, you listen good, Sinclair. If I let you live tonight, you don't know who put this pain on you. Sheriff's not gonna help—or care—so don't bother. But if you talk to *anybody*, that sister of yours? I'm gonna *own* her."

Ready. Get ready for another kick. But it doesn't come—only pain, and blood trickling everywhere, and stars that turn out in a bunch, like on a Christmas tree.

I TRY TO OPEN MY eyes, but only one works. A bird calls from far away, and another answers. I didn't think birds chirp this late. Never told Jess I love her. Don't know if I'm dead or alive. Probably close to both.

"Miss?" a voice from somewhere says. "Can you hear me? I'm manager of The Shine-A-Mite. I need your phone number, so we can call your people. Want an ambulance? Surely looks like you can use one."

I want to shake my head, but it won't shake. "No... ambulance. Can't pay." I mumble my phone number though lips that aren't mine. It must come out okay, because nobody asks again.

Something's shoved under my head. Can't make it out; soft and not soft. "Be careful in case her neck's broke," someone with a mountain accent says.

A car door slams and another; then gravelly footsteps. "Violette, what kind of mess you in now?"

"Ma-ma?" *I... can't see... left eye broke. Gotta say I love you, case I die.*

A body's crying real hard. Don't think it's me. "J... Jess?"

"I'm here, Vi. I'm right here. Don't you worry about a thing."

I gotta get up and help Jess 'cause she's upset, but something's bound me to the asphalt. I can make out cigarette butts and glass shards. But what's holding me? It's gum. Gum in my hair; a final insult. Even more than Dale beating me to death.

Two people hoist me on legs that can't carry my weight. Something stinks; vomit. A deep voice says, "This girl needs a hospital real bad. She could up and die on you."

A person who's gotta be Jessie says, "Thanks, mister, but I'll take good care of her."

A body won't shut up moaning, and I think it's me.

Jessie sort of folds me into the car, and lots of those stars come in too.

"I'm gonna drive slow as I can, Vi. Don't want to shake you up more'n necessary."

Mmp.

"Lord. Lord," a faraway sounding Mama says. "The death of us all."

After forever, the car stops, and a door opens. My eyes are a throbbing wound. *Please, Jesus, let it be dark again.*

The Jessie voice says, "Think you can get in the house, if I help you?"

My lips aren't lips anymore. "Mm-hm."

"Sorry to drag you like this, Vi."

Somebody makes me collapse on my bed. Pain eats me alive. "Jess, you still here?"

"I'm here, sis. I won't leave you."

"Gotta tell you."

"Vi, tell me later. You need to save your energy."

"No, now. Now."

"Okay, Vi. Okay." She takes my hand and holds it tight.

"Jess, I love you."

"I love you, too, Vi. Truly. Now I'm gonna help get you well. Just wait and see."

10

"HOW'S SHE DOING?" A VOICE from far away says.

"Still hard to tell. She's been in and out all day, kind of like the last two."

"In and out," says somebody who sounds like me.

A giant hand covers mine. "You wakin' up, Vi?"

"Think so."

"You... guys been friends a long time, Junior," a Jessie voice says.

I nod.

"Yeah. Me and Violette, we been tight since we were knee-high to an Ozark Howler. She's always had my back, a whole lot more'n most of my guy friends. Hell, we took care of each other since the day she punched out Donny McDuffie in kindergarten for calling me a fat redneck. Gave him the bloodiest nose I ever saw, at least from a girl."

"She's lucky," the Jessie voice whispers. "Luckier than most people."

"Well... we both are," the Junie voice says.

My mind's back in old times. And then it isn't. I open my eyes.

"There you are, Violette. You've had us all worried," Doc says, putting her stethoscope around her neck.

"Doc? You're here too."

Something clears in my brain like sun after fog. Raising my hand to the bad eye, I touch stitches and rough skin. "It was you fixed my eye and put me back together."

She squeezes my arm. "So you remember. That's a good sign."

"Why'd you help?"

"Because you needed me, and I could do it."

"Doc, I... thank you." No other words. No more strength.

"We don't have to talk about anything now. I have an idea of how you feel, and you may be emotional for a while, but here's the important thing: You'll be good as new when the healing's done. No scars. No permanent internal damage. You had some rib involvement but no breaks. There's not too much difference treating dogs, or cows, or people. You'll realize that more clearly when you're in vet school. I'll tell you all this again when you're more awake."

I try hard to talk but can't. But I smile and wipe a tear from my left eye. The one that Doc fixed.

* * *

"THIS COULD BECOME A REAL good habit," I tell Jessie when she totes in a tray with bacon that I could smell from the kitchen. And two of the prettiest eggs in the world staring up at me. And coffee. Mama's steaming coffee.

"How's my patient this morning, Dr. Vet-to-be?"

"Pretty much okay, Jess," I say, my voice almost normal. "It's like a miracle how a week can put so much pain behind you, that and what you did for me."

"It's what sisters do," she says. "But don't forget about Doc's help."

"What can I do to repay her, Jessie? It's almost all I think of; that and what you did."

"Look, sis, she doesn't want to be paid. She said she wanted to help you—in the circumstance—like she put it. It was me who called her. I didn't know what to do; you were so worked up about not going to the hospital, being so afraid of Dale and all."

"Jessie, I…"

"Let me finish. You need to know what happened now you're better; why we did what we did."

I lean back on my pillow, a signal for Jess to go on.

"Doc told us to wait about doing anything till she got here. She arrived with her bag all full of stuff and got to work. Felt like it took forever, but I never seen… saw anybody more careful. I helped her when she called for it."

I nod. "Junior told me he was here, but I can't get a straight answer from him about what happened that night."

"Junior, he was so good with Mama. She… she was awful upset. Went on and on about her firstborn child and all that. Junior… well, like I said, he was real good with her. Quieted her down. Even made her laugh with old stories about you and him."

Jessie's still for a minute, and I think she's done, but she's not.

"When Doc was finished, we—me, and Junior, even Mama— took an oath never to tell who fixed you up, her maybe getting in trouble with the vet board and all. Doc, she didn't ask us to. We just thought it was the thing to do."

"Well, even though I'm kind of embarrassed by it all, I'm glad you told me."

Jessie's smile lets me look straight into her heart. "Yeah, I thought you would. Now can I help you anymore? Seth and me... Seth and I... are taking off to the state fair in Springfield today."

"No, y'all have fun, and tell him hi for me."

"Of course I will."

In a few minutes, I hear car wheels squeal and the front door slam. They're gone. It's time to get on with things, and that means finally looking hard in the mirror. "Hey, Mama?"

"What's wrong," she hollers, then rushes into the bathroom. "You okay, Violette?"

"Yeah, didn't mean to scare you. I... I just didn't want to look at my face alone. Been trying to put it off."

Mama plants her hands on her hips. "Violette, you look fine for what happened to you last week. Go ahead, be brave, and look straight on in that mirror."

My hands start to ache. I look down and realize they've gripped the sink top so tight, they might as well be connected to it. "I... just can't."

"Child, I know how you feel," she says in a softer voice than I've heard from her in years. "Something like this happened to a... good friend of mine once. She found the best thing was to get it over with. Just look in the mirror. And believe me, your face isn't as bad as you think."

"I'll try."

"Good."

The sink's cold on my belly when I lean against it, and my eyes are clamped shut in front of the scratched mirror of the old medicine chest. When I open them real slow, a girl with two black eyes and a swollen and bruised face stares back. Funny that the inside wounds, like grief and sorrow, show right through my eyes, and I wonder if other people see it. "Well, you're right, Mama," I say. "It's still me even after being beat so bad, but inside my mouth is raw as field-dressed venison."

"Yeah, but like Doc said, you were lucky not to lose any teeth. My friend lost some and got her nose broke too. I'm grateful the same didn't happen to you."

"Who was your friend, Mama? I don't recall that story."

"Oh, Violette, it was a coon's age. I can't hardly remember any of the particulars."

I look at my mama and get the notion she's somewhere, someplace else. But after a few seconds she says, "See? That wasn't bad as you reckoned, was it?"

"No, it wasn't." I want to hug her but don't.

"Happy to oblige," she says and puts her arm out like maybe she's gonna hug me, but she doesn't. "I'm making a jug of iced tea, child. You want some?"

"Sure, uh, I'd love a glass. Think I'll give Junior a call too," I say, snagging my phone off the hall table.

Five rings, then he picks up. "Hey, Vi. How you feeling?"

"Better each day, Junie. You want to get a coffee?"

"Uh, can't do it now. Hold on a minute." I hear a shuffling noise on the other end, and then a door slams. "Vi?"

"Yeah, what's up?"

"Aw, it's Jake again. More meth trouble. Only this time, he's really gone and done it. Him and some other guys were cooking in the hills? Went and blew up the shack and one of them got burned real bad; had to be airlifted to Springfield. The rest are in jail over in Blaylock. My folks are real torn up, because this'll probably mean more than juvie."

"Oh, man. That sucks, Junie. I've never seen jail straighten anybody out. Around here, anyway."

"Yeah, so I gotta go be with Maw and Daddy. They need me about now, and Jake too, I guess. One thing I need to tell you, though; probably something Doc should know. Jake, he told me this morning word's out about those dogfights lined up to start again on Hog Back. He's got no idea about the ringleader, but word's out it's not just local this time. Big money's involved, a syndicate of some kind investing in it. Like from Kansas City. A real big town anyway."

Hearing his news makes me shiver. There's enough meanness to go around without that kind of cruelty. "It'll upset her, Junie, but I'll give Doc the message. She does need to know about it. Uh, listen, tell your folks I'm thinking of them."

"Will do. Later, Vi."

"Yeah. Later."

"WAKE UP, VIOLETTE." MAMA GIVES my shoulder a little shake. "You been asleep ever since you had that iced tea this morning. How about toting the trash bags to the dump now you've had a rest? Be good for you to get up and move around a little. Jessie and Seth won't be home from Springfield till late, and it's almost dark. C'mon now; there's only two of them—bags—I mean, but they're nasty with all the vegetables I put up yesterday. I'm not about to get rats around here."

"Okay. I'll try."

"I'll trundle the bags to the truck and put them in. That'll ease things for you, won't it? They're not too heavy," she adds, saying it more to ease herself than me, I think.

"It will. Thanks, Mama."

11

EVEN IF YOU DON'T KNOW where it is, the dump gives off such a vile odor it's easy to find. I park the truck close as I dare to the smoldering garbage pile, scan the dismal scene, and shudder. *Why did I agree to carry this trash over here tonight? It could have waited till morning.*

A powerful beam in the rearview mirror catches my attention quick. I rub my eyes and strain to see beyond the glare, but all I can make out are two truck-high headlights coming on fast. I brace myself, ready to jump out before my truck's shoved in the dump fire.

The vehicle tears up to my tailgate but doesn't touch it. The blazing lights put me in mind of a UFO ready to take me over— that is, if I believed in UFOs. Reaching for the door handle, I open it, then slam the thing shut again. *What should I do? I'm trapped.*

A door bangs shut behind me, and I can make out a figure lumbering to my window. A man, shadows from the firelight flickering on his bald head, pounds on the glass. "So y'all healed up and fixin' for the next hurt—or worse?"

The voice is too familiar.

I open my window the tiniest crack. "I'm sick of your threats, Dale, and I'm sick of you."

I've got no answer for why I'm putting myself in this kind of danger sassin' him. But I'm so tired of his orneriness, and I'm hurting inside and out, and I'm fed up with being called names, and... I guess that's all, but it's enough.

"You're gonna get sicker of me before this night's spent. Reason being I got me a... enforcer settin' there in the truck. Maybe you'd like *him* better. He's along in case I decide to do some hard work, like dig a grave, or some such."

"You know what, Dale? Saying ignorant stuff like that is just plain dumb, and the only person looks that way is you."

Before he can answer, the passenger door of Dale's truck opens. Dale snarls, "Stay where you are, Rucker. I'm not ready for you yet."

"Aw, c'mon," the guy bellyaches, but closes the door.

I smirk at Dale and wish there was real courage behind it. "So now you're following a defenseless girl to the dump? You gotta have way too much time on your hands."

He hawks up spit and blasts the ground with it. "You're a fool, Sinclair. A damn fool."

"No, you're the fool, Dale, and a damn bully boy. You beat me up, then threaten me again. What's wrong with you? Your mama surely didn't raise you right."

Dale puts a look of pure hate on me. "You ain't good enough to even mention my mama."

He glances back at his truck. "Rucker, get your ass on over here. It's time."

Dale glares at me, grabs the handle, and then pops open my door.

I forgot to relock it! We stare at each other a second, then I dive to the passenger seat and jerk open the door handle. Leaping out of the truck, I land on my right side, fetching back all those pain stars from when I was Dale-beat. *Oh, my God. I can't hardly move.* Somebody gives a sob. Must be me.

"Got the rope?" Dale hollers from around my truck.

"Right here in my hand," Rucker mumbles, like he has a smoke dangling from his mouth.

"Well, come on, then. Let's get this over with. Make my maw in Heaven real… satisfied."

Get up. Get up, Vi. No way you're gonna let these creeps win. Balancing on my knees, I push hard with my left arm, wobble, and stand up. With Dale between his truck and me, and Rucker looming on my right, I'm trapped. But maybe I can squeeze between the fire and my truck. I back up, and heat from the flames warms my heels.

"You get your sweet self on over to Daddy," Dale huffs, then lunges at me.

I skinny on through the airspace at my left. Licks of fire touch my toes, and scorched rubber from my flip-flop soles stings my nose. A hand grabs my shoulder, but I shake it off, then scream the loudest, most bloodcurdling sound I've ever made or heard.

"Hell. Almost got her," Rucker bellyaches again.

I hate this guy.

"Let's go," Dale yells. "Let her go!"

"What you talking about, Dale? You crazy? I pretty near snagged her."

"Somebody's coming. We can't get her in time, you moron. In the truck. Now!"

Dale opens his door. "We ain't finished with you, Sinclair. Consider this a little extra time, kinda like on death row. Gives you more time to think on what's coming."

"Well, *hell*," Rucker complains again. He punches my side door with his fist and dashes to Dale's truck. It backs up, lurches forward, and passes the oncoming car. It rockets on down Dump Road and is gone.

Standing in stinking garbage, I survey this filthy place. It feels full of death, and I shudder, picturing me sprawled on top of it. My whole body's in pain, but it's fear tearing me apart.

I wipe away hot tears; not time to cry yet. Hobbling to the back of the truck, I hoist the two bags and drop them at the creeping fire's edge. I'm done and hauling ass out of here.

A sliver of moon follows me home and hangs over Mama's car when I rumble on in behind it. Whole world's still as death after I shut off the engine, but for a barn owl hooting off in the distance. Getting ready to go hunting; pretty much like I was hunted a bit ago. I shiver and cross my arms over my smoke-filled T-shirt. *Only one way to get in the house, Vi. Might as well get it over with.*

I slip from the truck quiet as possible and push down the lock button. Heart battering my chest to bits, I gulp a huge breath of nighttime air, pound across the yard and hurl myself up the front steps. *Thank Jesus the door's unlocked.* I throw the deadbolt and sink to the floor, my side screaming, in case I forgot it was hurt bad.

Please God, if You're up there, I need help real bad. Don't think I can do this on my own. Can't even keep myself safe, let alone Jessie and Mama. I'd appreciate any assistance you could give. Thank you.

12

I SNAP AWAKE. MY LITTLE alarm clock says two-seventeen. Our room's dark as the inside of Collier's Coal Mine. My side throbs, and my T-shirt sticks to my sweaty back. Clammy cold's settling over me, and I shiver hard.

Suddenly a shadowy figure sneaks into my head, and I know who it is. Rucker. Rucker Hicks. The dump guy in Dale's truck earlier tonight. The guy whose picture I saw hanging over the receptionist's desk at the sheriff's office. The guy who was arrested for bank robbery, arson—and dogfighting. The guy who's the answer to my troubles with Dale. If I'm smart!

Holding onto my side, I inch out of bed and fire up Doc's hand-me-down computer that me and Jess share. When I google *Missouri's Most Wanted List*, there's nothing about Hicks. But since these two creeps hang together, that *could* include dogfights. The only chance I can see to save Jessie, and Mama, and me, is getting Dale on dogfight charges that'll send him over to the Jeff City Correction Center for a long time. A strange sensation bubbles up from my toes, and it feels an awful lot like hope.

"Junie, answer. Please."

"Hey, Vi," he says after a bunch of rings. His voice is gravel. "What's goin' on so early? Jeez, sun's not even up."

"Yeah, sorry, but I need to talk to you right away. Been awake since two-thirty. Couldn't hardly wait till now. I got a notion that could maybe save us from Dale. Can we meet up pretty soon?"

"Sure." He clears his throat. "Let's meet at the Shine. I can't get there before six anyway. Gotta take a shower, then head off to work right soon after."

"Okay. Thanks. This is my day off."

"See ya over there."

A whiff of fried bacon slams me in the nose when I open the café door about an hour later. I slide in on the chilly vinyl seat. "Hiya, Junie."

"Hey, Vi. Got you a coffee."

"Great. Thanks. How's everything at home?"

"Pretty quiet. Just waiting on Judge Sallee to collect more information, but we think Jake's gonna squeak by again—you know, on account of the kin connection."

"Well, if I could have a kin judge take care of Dale, I'd do it in a heartbeat and never look back."

I hate that about myself.

He stares at me real hard. "All right, Vi, what's going on? And how do you feel? Uh, I've missed seeing your mug, so talk to me."

"I'm okay. Doc says I'm getting better all the time. Still pretty tired's about it." I'm not talking about how my side really feels till I lay my idea on him. Scooting my butt to the edge of the seat, I prop my elbows on the table, look around, and lower my voice. "I got a plan to deal with Dale, and it goes like this."

JUNIOR LISTENS AND DOESN'T INTERRUPT, which is a pretty bad sign. Finally, he takes off his St. Louis Cardinals cap and turns it upside-down on the table. "What the hell you talking about, Vi? Trying to snag these guys and all. You just finish telling me how Dale and that Hicks dude tried to kidnap you last night? Hicks *will* kill you, and it'll make his day shine. You're putting yourself in trouble so deep it's guaranteed to get you dead. Hell, you don't know who you're messing with here."

"No, I don't, so talk to me."

He folds his huge hands on the table next to his cap and sort of scans my face. "This Hicks guy's like a super-sized Dale, and I'm not talking body weight here. He's been to the big house for stuff like armed robbery and I think arson. He's dangerous and connected to a world of bad guys you don't want to know. Jake, he's had some... contacts with him, I guess you'd say. I don't think Rucker cooks, but he sure uses and sells, and that's where he's crossed paths with my brother, who says he's scarier than the devil himself."

"Weird I never heard tell of him before now. Does he live around here?"

Junior runs his index finger around the rim of his cup and shakes his head. "Not so weird. Law's always looking for him, but he never gets caught these days."

"Is he a crony of the sheriff? Must be if he never gets arrested anymore."

"Can't say as I know, but I wouldn't be surprised. Old Rucker, he just comes and goes, like the bad weather my daddy's always predicting. But I hear from Jake he's waist-deep in the dogs with this syndicate—you know—folks from out of the area. Big city money guys who'd shoot you and bury you in a shallow grave without one look back except to see if you're dead enough."

"Yeah, Junior, but we gotta keep in mind something real important: Rucker's not *our* bad guy. He's the way we *get* to our bad guy. We need to watch *both* their sorry asses, then work out a plan to catch them red-handed."

Junior takes a swig of coffee, then sets the thick white mug down hard. "How we gonna do that? Like I said, you never know where Rucker is."

"He is where Dale is. You shoulda heard Dale bossing him around at the dump, Junie. Dale's the boss, not Rucker." I stop a second and let Junior chew that over. "What about we go up Hog Back, snoop around, and try to find the actual dogfight place."

"You sure as hell don't need to be gallivanting around up there, Miz Sinclair. You and Jessie tried it, and look how that turned out for you."

My insides seize up. "I feel real bad about putting Jess in danger. That was… thoughtless of me, and I won't take her back up there under any conditions."

Junior puffs out a big breath and looks out the window. I follow his gaze. Sun's starting to come up, and there's that soft light between dark and daytime. I've always liked this time of morning; fresh and dewy, like things are starting over. All new, even if they were bad the day before.

Junior turns back to me and clasps his hands on the scarred Formica table. "Look, I ain't saying that trying to find a link between those two jerk-offs isn't a good idea. And nailing them with the dogs is basically smart, if you don't count getting your butt stomped. But going up there with those fights starting right away? People you don't want to mess with are gonna be crawling all over the place. You could get to that shallow grave quicker than a toad in a tornado." Junior looks at his folded hands, a sure sign something I won't like is coming. "I been mulling a thought over and don't want you to get mad."

"What?"

"It's just that… I think you need to… examine why you put yourself in danger all the time, Vi. It's like you got to prove something over and over, even when it puts you at… unnecessary risk. *Especially* when it does, like the way you talked to Dale right after he beat you up. That's no reasonable way to act." He stares at his nearly empty cup. "And about your daddy."

"Junie—"

"No. Hear me out. You *gotta* give up on tracking down his killer. Everybody knows it was Dale. Okay? No use getting dead over something you can't change. Let it *go!*"

"Junie—"

"Vi," he says, so gentle. "I think you… act like you do because of what happened in seventh grade. With Brandy. But bad as that was, you can't let it, like, take you over, or change who you are, or… get you killed. That serves no purpose. None at all."

Hot tears threaten to tumble down my cheeks. I look at the last drops of coffee in my cup instead of Junie's eyes. "But this is the *only* way I know to save us from Dale. I mean, without the law or Uncle Gray's help, what can I do? I *have* to get something on him. And as much as I'm hurt by my daddy's murder, that's not what

I was even *looking* for. It just kind of happened when I started to poke around."

Junior stares at me hard, then shakes his head. Him not saying anything rattles me.

"Well, I'll think on what you said, Junie. I really will."

"Promise me you'll do that, Vi? Before I leave you today?"

"I promise to stay as safe as I can when you're not with me. That okay?"

"Knowing you, I guess it'll have to do."

But I'm going up anyway. Today, on my day off. Nobody's gonna stop me from saving my family—and myself.

13

SOME OF THOSE BLACK SPOTS are back. They swirl in front of my eyes and make it hard to drive. And even worse, that shallow grave warning Junie put on me back at the Shine half an hour ago keeps roaming around in my head. When I turn onto the winding road that leads up Hog Back, my body shudders. This journey could get me dead quick.

Once on the mountain, I push away the notion that I'm too close to Woodbine land. I need to concentrate on clues, but what kind? Driving slow, I search hard for telltale signs of folks' activity where none should be. The mostly wild countryside is shot through with low-slung witch hazel trees under canopies of hawthorn and hickory. Wild ginger and ground ivy creep around and along tree trunks, clashing for root space. Every so often, in a spot touched by the sun, horseweed unwraps its raggedy flowers to flies and wasps.

After an hour or so of trailing nothing but my imagination, the sun's about three feet over my head, my rib has to be splintered, and the pain in my face won't stop screaming. I've pretty near covered this whole place except for Woodbine property. My mama didn't raise no fools who have to be warned twice by the law to keep away. It's time to traipse on down Hog Back Mountain and give up this crazy notion.

I stop the truck and let the engine idle a second to rest my head on the steering wheel, but something curious ahead gets my attention. A pretty little lane's almost covered by overhanging bushes on each side. But a lot of the leaves and some branches have been beat down or ripped. Why? Because traffic goes through there all the time, that's why. I sit in the truck with my mouth hanging open while my backbone turns to ice and the hair on my neck stands straight up.

I put the truck in gear and drive molasses-slow through the ripped-up curtain of green. There's nothing suspicious around here. I'm wasting my time. But when I pass a meadow, my heart does a flip. Oh, my God. What about that trail? The one that cuts the meadow in half and looks worn down. Worn down by lots of feet.

Parking as far off the road as possible, I sit a second to ponder my choices. I don't want to get out where I could get myself killed. I do want to stay inside where it's safe. But I've come this far. *Get out. You have to take care of your family.* Which is only part true, because something else deep inside's making me do it, like Junie said a couple of hours ago.

Holding my side tight as possible, I step out and listen hard. Nothing but high summer sounds of birds warbling and a breeze rustling leaves. Before I cross the narrow road, I pause and look both ways.

The meadow is long but not too wide. The trek across takes me to a double barbed wire fence attached to a padlocked metal gate at the tree line. A long electrical box on a pole is next to the gate frame. Why would you use electricity around here? If the sheriff's trying to find a dogfighting ring, that box could be a dead giveaway. *Come on*, I think. Sheriff Fletcher damn well knows the fight location.

Hauling my aching body over the gate, I try to clear all thoughts of getting killed out of my mind. A tacked-up, hand-painted sign on a tall white pine screams at me: *What You See Here, Hear Here, Stays Here!* That's super creepy.

How far back in the woods am I gonna go? I need to be reasonable for once, like Junie says. Seems like I've walked about five minutes past that sign, so it's time to stop again. I root myself to the weedy ground and listen. Only a few birds call, and leaves rustle against each other in the slight breeze. But there's something else; an undertone in the air. Buzzing. Lots of it. Must be a beehive close by. *Huh-uh.* It's flies swarming in that high grass. Slipping closer, I see nothing. *It's your imagination. Get outta here. Okay, maybe two steps closer won't hurt.*

"Oh, my God!"

Dead dog. In the weeds. Tan with black markings. Pit bull or mix of one and very young. Poor thing's caked with dried saliva and blood. Its lips and eyes are bloody wounds. A deep gash is carved into its right flank. The paws are still oozing, so it must have just died.

A rush of heat flashes through me. *Gotta get out of here.* I see enough cruelty to animals at Doc's to last a lifetime. I've examined too many blameless animals that suffer pain and death from humans who are inhumane: heartless, and brutal, and violent. *Get away, and don't look back. Don't think back. Never come to this terrible place again.* My body is total adrenaline as I book it to the truck. Sweat drops off my chin and trickles down my back. Gasping in humid air, I know I'm out of control. Because of the dead dog. And because of what's happening to me. And to Mama and Jess.

Just past the creepy sign that warns people not to talk about what they see up here, a thought, in neon, flashes into my mind: When an animal's dead, oozing stops or is so slow that one drip takes forever. This was a lot faster than I've seen on dead animals at Doc's. I come to a standstill so fast I almost lose my balance, jerking my right side. Suddenly those same pain stars come on out, but I ignore them. *I have to go back to that pup. Fast.*

Clearing everything from my mind, I concentrate on the dog. If it's alive, maybe I can help keep it that way. Just like Doc would. Limping along, holding my side, I can't go so fast but do the best I can.

Close to where I thought I saw the dog, I slow way down. *Look for a swarm of flies. Listen too.* There! I ease myself onto the ground, shoo the black buzzing mass away, and touch the dog gentle as a feather. Still warm, but no heartbeat that I can find. Wish I had a stethoscope. Hand to its mouth; no breath. Eyes so wounded, I can't tell anything from them. Not getting any blinking.

I stroke its back. "Little one, I don't think I can help you." And then I feel, rather than see, a slight tail movement. "Oh! You gave me such a start. Hurt this bad, you could bite and not even know it. But I know what *Doc* would do. She'd try to save you, and I will too."

The wounded animal cracks open a blood-caked eye.

"I think you're trying to focus on my voice, puppy. I'm a friend, here to rescue you—somehow."

The dog shudders slightly and closes its eye. "Oh, no. Don't die. Doc can fix you up too." An almost invisible tail wag. "You're still with me; stay with me."

I swipe at my sweat-covered face, flies now attacking my eyes. How do I get this dog moved? Must be about thirty pounds. I don't have anything like a stretcher, and it won't tolerate being carried. What can I use? What's in the truck? Nothing. No. There is! Aunt Zinnie's tablecloth. The one Mama told me to take back to her the night I was beat up. I stroke the dog's fur again. "Maybe I can drag you on it. Nobody's deserting you again, if *I* can help it."

As I stand to go, the dog whimpers like a newborn kitten mewling. "I know you're afraid I'm leaving, but I'll be back soon. Promise."

My legs are so weak, I'm afraid they're not going to support me for long. Wobbling a mite, I hold onto my side and stare down at the pathetic puppy I'm trying to save. "C'mon, Vi. You can do this. His life is in your hands."

I turn, hoping hard I can make it to the truck then back to the dog without collapsing. When I reach the gate, I search for a place to drag the dog through and find one. Pretty sure I can just squeeze him between those two support poles.

Gnats attack my eyes, and horseflies divebomb my head, but I trek on toward the truck

Soon as I reach it, I say a prayer. *Please let the tablecloth still be there.* Almost afraid to look, I unlock the door and scan the back floor. There it is, right where I put it a week ago, a lifetime ago. I grab it up and slam the door. Slippery grasses wind around my legs like garter snakes, and thistle thorns rip my clothes. Panic, and despair, and hope, tear at my heart.

When I throw myself on the ground next to the dog, piercing pain tears through my side. *Ignore it, Vi. That's what Doc would do.* Putting my face low to the pup's head, I whisper, "I'm back, little one, like I promised. Can you open your eyes again? You still with me?" *Please let him be.* Another tail thump gives me the answer. "This is gonna hurt. Sorry. Let me tuck the cloth under you. Now a little push. And one more. Gentle, gentle. And a tiny roll. Oh. You're a girl. You stay alive now, little girl. Hear? You and me got a Get Out of Hell Pass."

"I FEEL ABOUT A HUNDRED years old pulling you through these weeds so slow," I tell the passed-out dog. "Reckon we're about halfway there. Let me check your pulse." A thrill of terror charges through me. Her heart's beating, just barely. "You're so hot. If only I had some water to cool you down. Problem is we couldn't stop for long now, anyway, see? If the fight guys come, they'll kill us both. Make sure we're never found."

Our trip through the woods is made slower by me having to change directions to keep the pup away from ruts, and tree stumps, and such. Sweat floods my face and neck. My hands are slippery, and I have to wipe them on my shorts every few minutes. But when we reach the open meadow and I see the truck, my spirit lightens way up.

The pup and I pretty near fly to the door. Problem is my hands are shaking so bad, I can't hardly get the key in the lock. Finally, when the lock opens, tears mix with sweat, and I don't know which is which, and I don't care neither. "Here we are, baby; almost safe," I say, so soft. "Gotta use my leg muscles. Gonna lift you. Now." She makes no sound when I lay her on the floor, and her head lolls from side to side. Aunt Zinnie's tablecloth is scarlet. I'll worry about that later.

A voice made of gravel and concrete yells, "Hey, you! Whaddya up to?"

I shut the passenger door and turn around like I've got all the time in the world, even though I'm basically sure we're dead. A middle-aged man with a pock-scarred face and a long ponytail stares me down. I try to find my voice. "Who're you?"

He holds up a tattoo-covered arm, balls up a fist, and then puts it on his hip. His other hand holds a serious firearm. A machine-gun-type weapon. "Who am I? Who're *you*? You're the trespasser, not me. I own this land, for your information. I'll ask you one more time before I hurt you. What the hell you doing here?"

"Nothing, mister; I'm leaving's what I'm doing." I walk around the truck, open my door, scoot in, and start the engine.

Akk, akk, akk. Short bursts of fire power explode over my truck. *What the hell? He's shooting!*

Tattoo Arms dashes alongside the truck and aims the weapon straight at my head. "Get on out of there. Now."

"Okay, I'm out."

"Because you're female, I'll ask one more time before I commence shooting again. Only this time it ain't gonna be a warning shot. What're you doing on my land?"

I raise my quaking arms over my head. "Okay, I'll tell you. I was just embarrassed is all. I had to pee bad, looked around and didn't see anybody, so I... well, I did my business and about then you showed up. Hey, I'm real sorry, but you know how it is, when nature calls and all." I scrunch up my face and shrug, hoping I look cute.

The man puts a hard stare on me, then slowly lowers his gun. "It's a good thing for you I got a wife and three daughters, so I *do* know how that is. Get on with you, and next time do your business someplace else, you hear?"

"Yes, sir. And thank you mightily for being so understanding."

He takes off his John Deere cap and returns it to exactly where it was on his head. *I wonder why guys do that,* runs through my mind: ridiculous at a time like this. I duck my head below the dash so he can't see my lips move. "Come on, baby. Let's get you to the hospital."

14

THE DOG HASN'T STIRRED SINCE we left the mountain. Sweat stings my eyes so bad I can't hardly see. "Stay with me, pup. We're almost there. Doc'll fix you up." I hope it isn't a promise we can't keep. I drive too quick into the clinic parking lot. "Where's Doc, Nedda?" I yell to the Blaylock Clinic receptionist.

"Oh, hey, Vi. I think you just missed her."

"I've got a dying dog in my truck, and she has to be looked at now. Can't wait."

"Well, check the parking lot, and see if she's still here. Last I saw of her, she was headed home."

I rush out the back door. Her truck, blinker on, is ready to pull out into the street as soon as a tractor creeps by. "Doc! Doc!" Her window's up, and she's moving forward bit by bit. "Please, Doc!" I scream, hobbling toward her. "Doc! Doc! Help!" The truck lurches, and the brake lights turn off. I hope I don't faint.

She opens the door and jumps out. "Vi. Violette. What's wrong?"

DOC REMOVES HER LATEX GLOVES with a *snap* and uncovers her hair. "That's about all we can do for her now. If she pulls through, she'll be a miracle dog. You need to prepare yourself, Vi."

I nod and glance at the wall clock. "Can't believe what all you did for her these past three hours." Reaching under the blankets, I pet the dog's fur, so soft since she was cleaned up for surgery.

Doc checks the pup's IV, then gives me a smile full of weariness. "Zach'll keep a good watch over her through the night, so don't worry about that, and I'll call you first thing tomorrow morning. Now, let me look at you."

"I'm okay," I lie. "Only thing that twinges is my rib."

"Let's do an X-ray to see what's up since you lifted her into the truck. It's the main thing I'm still concerned about at this point."

A fish fillet knife plunging into my side and twisting for good measure: that's what it feels like to get on the x-ray table. As the machine takes pictures of my rib, all I can think of is the puppy. I know I can't have her because Mama will never agree, like all the other times she said no when I begged for one. But in my heart this dog will always be mine, and I'll be hers. Even if she doesn't live through the night, we're still each other's.

Doc's voice takes me away from Mama's lack of caring. "Look, I know why you lifted her, and I would have done the same. But you've sustained some real damage by doing so. Your rib's moved a bit from the strain, so it's going to take more time to mend. In the meantime, I want you to pick up nothing—and I mean nothing— or there could be *permanent* damage. Got it?"

"Got it, Doc. And I'll be good, promise."

"You *have* to be. Tell your baby good night now. Go home and rest. And, Vi? What you did today for this poor animal at that hellish place is nothing short of heroic. I'm as proud of you as if you were my own daughter."

Heat rushes to my face. "Thank… thank you, Doc." I study my old black flip-flops like I never saw them before. "That's the nicest thing anyone's ever said to me."

"Then it's time you hear something nice. You're a fine young woman with all the right stuff to make a success of your life. In some ways, you remind me of me at your age." She looks down and studies her shoes for a second too. "It can be tough going through the teen years, especially around here where lots of folks have fixed ideas about right and wrong. As for me, I was kind of a wild kid living in the Arkansas Ozarks; got into a little trouble occasionally. To be honest, more than occasionally."

I feel my eyes go wide. "You?"

She rubs her covered-up motorcycle tattoo, the one I've seen only once when she had to roll up her sleeve because it got all bloody. "Yep. I tended to like boys and alcohol too much. It took a special teacher and my grandmother to step in and, well, show they cared. Not sure where I'd be without them." She puts her hand on my shoulder and squeezes it. I bet she won't mention any of this again. But what she's said is enough.

When Doc walks out of the Trauma Room, I gaze back at the sedated dog. I'm filled with love and awe that she's had the will to hang on this long. I tuck the blanket tighter around her back, then put my mouth to the top of her ear. "Stay with us, girl. I need you as much as you need me, maybe more." And I kiss the silky fur between her ears.

MAMA'S CAR IS GONE WHEN I pull up behind her spot at the edge of the front door. I don't even feel guilty about being glad she's not here. I want to tell Jess all about the puppy and hurry to the door. "Hey, Jess," I call. "You here? Gotta tell you what happened today."

"In the kitchen, working on my damn cheerleading outfit. This time the hem's coming unraveled."

"Want me to fix it?"

"Maybe, but I'll try first."

"Give me a shout if you need some help. Uh, I got some news about a puppy I saved. Want to hear?"

"A puppy! Yeah."

I sit down and watch Jess struggle with needle and thread. "Okay. Here's what happened." But I don't get very far in the telling, because soon as I get to searching alone for the dogfight area, Jessie flings her costume on the table. "Before you go on, I gotta ask you a question. Why do you put yourself in this kind of danger all the time? I mean, I get it about trying to find something on Dale. That makes sense. But going up Hog Back alone? What are you thinking?"

"Jess, Junie already—"

"No. Don't give me no… zany excuses, Vi. Way you acted is plain… ignorant's what it is. Now, I want to hear about the puppy and all. But I want my sister more. That's all I'm gonna say." She pushes her hair back, and I know something else is coming. "Except I'm telling Junior."

"I'm going to tell him myself, Jess. And me and him, we've already talked about me… taking risks, unnecessary ones, if you want to know the truth."

"Then why—" Jessie puts a look on me, her eyes fiery.

"You already *know* why. I *have* to get something on Dale. *Tell* me if you see another way. Well, come on." I'm getting madder at my sister by the second. Why doesn't she get it? And Junie too? I stick my chin out real far but hate myself for getting mad at Jess.

The fire's gone out of her. When she looks at me, her eyes hold nothing but worry. "I just don't want to lose you again, Vi. And this time it could be for good."

I put my head down 'cause tears are close. "Thanks, Jess. But the law won't help me or any of us Sinclairs, seems like. And you know Sheriff Fletcher keeps getting elected. And Uncle Gray, he's useless. What can I do?" The fight's drained out of me too, and I'm tired.

Jessie says, "I don't know what to do. But we'll think of something. Junior too, okay? Together and not alone. Deal?"

"Deal." I love my sister more than I ever thought possible right this minute. Maybe what I promised is a lie. Maybe not. Suppose it all depends.

Jessie gives me a small smile. "Now tell me about the puppy."

15

THE BLAYLOCK CLINIC'S PARKING LOT'S empty as Mama's church on a campground revival night. Looks like I beat everyone this morning. Since I know Zack's already gone home from the night shift, I may as well hunker down in the truck till somebody with a key gets here. I fiddle with my phone, rummage through my briefcase, and worry about the pup for about twenty minutes until Nedda arrives.

"Hey, Nedda. I give her a sheepish smile. "Couldn't wait."

"Well, nobody'd blame you for that. I'll open up, and you go have a look-see."

My morning coffee lurches in my stomach. "Thanks."

Quiet and warm, the Trauma Room has a seriousness about it. My sneakers sound like combat boots treading across the tile floor to the puppy's cage. Still as death itself, she has an IV attached to her leg, and tubes are connected everywhere, same as yesterday. Trying to stay calm like a good vet, I wonder if a heart kicking out of your chest and legs that may not hold you up count as calm.

I turn on a low light over her crate. "Hi, baby. Let's find out what's going on." I can't see her breathing. I take the stethoscope from around my neck, but my hands are shaking so hard I'm scared I might drop it. When I listen, my heart crashes to the floor. No heartbeat. I reach under her blanket. Nothing. She's still warm, but... listen again. The stethoscope's slippery from sweat. I wipe it on my lab coat and put it to my ear. Wait. Something. A faint murmur. Again. A heartbeat. Slight, but there. "Stay with me, girl. You can do it, just like I did. We both have Doc to mend us."

I jump at a soft sound and glance behind me. "Doc. I didn't know you were here."

"You were so efficient, I didn't want to disturb the... medical practice I saw happening."

"Thanks, Doc. I... I thought she was gone, even listening through the scope. But now when I stroke her head, she tries to open an eye."

"This puppy knows you saved her, Vi. I'm absolutely sure of it. She has a long way to go, but since she held her own last night, that's a milestone. And how are *you* doing this morning?"

"Great. Wonderful. May be the best day of my life. All thanks to you."

"Vi—"

"I know she may not make it. But if she doesn't, at least she had a chance. You gave her that."

Doc treads silently across the room. "Now that you've done the initial check, Vi, let me look at her wounds." I step back, and she bends over the puppy. "The lines are all working. Let's give you a new IV, girl."

"I'll get it, Doc."

She glances at me and smiles. "I have an idea. My first call of the day is a visit to the Ferguson farm. Sick horse. Going out there will take your mind off the puppy."

"I'd like that. Mr. Ferguson, he's a nice man. I've chatted with him here at the clinic a couple times. I felt terribly sorry for him when you had to put down his sick old dog."

She smiles that little smile of hers, and I know she gets that I'm imitating the way she talks. "Let's put in a new IV for this baby of yours, then I'll gather my supplies, and we'll be off."

AFTER ABOUT A TWENTY-FIVE-MINUTE DRIVE, Doc says, "We're almost there. You ever been out this way?"

"Seems like I have, maybe once, to look at a hound dog. With my daddy."

"What happened to your father? That is, if you don't mind sharing it with me."

I shake my head no, though I really do mind. I tell her anyway. "Well, seven years ago, on Thanksgiving afternoon, he was out deer hunting with two of my uncles. Some hunter—we never found out who it was—must have thought Daddy was a deer and killed him. I was always told it was one shot, but a bit ago I heard it was more." Can't figure why I told Doc about there being more than one shot. Don't matter anyhow. Dead is dead.

I peek at Doc, to see her expression now I've told her, but she looks the same. "There's something I never got about it, though. He was decked out in orange—vest, hat, whole outfit. You wouldn't think it'd happen, would you, fitted out safe like he was? I've always been troubled by that part of the story."

"I'm so sorry. I can see you were close to him. You have my sympathy."

"Thanks, Doc." Everybody says the same thing whether they mean it or not, but with Doc? She means it. Only thing is, she didn't answer my question.

We turn onto a bumpy lane with an almost-dried-up streambed alongside it. The truck stirs up thick gravel dust. Dragonflies dart around us, and yellow butterflies flit above purple blooming thistle and tall grasses. "You hear dogs barking, Doc?"

"I do. Somebody must keep hunting hounds nearby. It's strange, though. These dogs aren't baying like hounds. Oh, well." She shrugs, and I can tell her thoughts are on to something else, probably Mr. Ferguson's horse.

We pull into the circle drive of an old stone and wood house a few minutes later. "Looks like the Fergusons have a pretty nice place, Doc. No trucks on blocks in the yard or washers and stuff on the front porch. You get a lot of that around here."

"True enough. Sometimes it makes my eyes tired just seeing that rubbish."

I don't answer, because our washer's on the front porch, and our dryer is the wind that whips everything stiff as a board on the clothes line.

Doc parks the truck, lowers her window, and waves to a slightly stooped man with thick gray hair and a kindly, weather-beaten face whose laugh lines speak of a happy nature. "Good morning, Doctor Campbell and Miss Sinclair. Two nice ladies today instead of one. You can't beat that," he says, ambling over to Doc's open door.

She flashes that wide smile that displays the dimple in her left cheek. "Thanks, Mr. Ferguson. Nice to know chivalry still exists."

"Well, thank *you* for getting here so fast. My horse, Barley, he doesn't look so good; not much energy these days, and yesterday he started doing something very strange." Mr. Ferguson gives us a small stare before going on, I suppose to make us understand how unusual the horse's symptoms are. "Well, it's like this. He began kicking at his stomach area."

"Colic." I put my hand to my mouth and look at Doc. "I shouldn't have said that. I'm real sorry."

"Actually, I think you're probably right, Vi. You've made a preliminary diagnosis, and I'd say it's a pretty good one. Would you please tell Mr. Ferguson what can be done to prevent this from happening in the future, *if* that's what it turns out to be?"

"Well," I say, scratching at a pretend mosquito bite. I need to stall for thinking time. "It's usually from an animal's eating moldy hay, or if it gets too hot—the animal, that is. Also, he ought to eat from the pasture if you can put him there."

"Right on all counts, Ms. Sinclair," she says.

I see Mr. Ferguson wink at Doc. "You can treat my animals any time, Violette."

"Yes, sir. Thank you."

Doc snags her bag from the back seat. "I'll get an antibiotic if you two want to go on to the barn." Her Crocs make a slapping sound across the gravel.

"Sure thing," Mr. Ferguson says, leading the way. He looks back and treats me to a smile that crinkles up the lines around his eyes. "You're on track to becoming a right fine vet, young lady."

"I appreciate that. Uh, Mr. Ferguson, can I ask you something?"

He raises his eyebrows, and I think it means yes.

I squint up at him and wish I hadn't said anything. "Last time we talked at the clinic? You asked me my last name, then said that my daddy was taken too soon. I know it was most likely a hunting accident, and talk is Dale Woodbine did it. But you see, I can't really find out anything about... *why* it happened. I mean, was it an accident, or did he have it in for my daddy?" I look down the path to see if Doc's returning from the truck, but she isn't yet.

Mr. Ferguson pushes back his International Harvester cap and glances away from me. "Well now, you ever talk to your mama or Gray Sinclair? They should be the ones—"

I put out my hand. "Sorry to interrupt, but I've tried, with my mama anyway, and can't get anywhere. Dale's on my case now, says he's gonna kill me—*and* my mama. And I gotta protect us, but I don't know why he's after us."

He frowns, and wrinkles deepen in his face. "You go to the sheriff with this?"

"Yes sir, soon as I heard. Told me it was a he said, she said thing and wasn't nothing to be done."

"Sounds like him, all right." He pauses, then says, "I'll talk to you about this, but you have to promise you'll tell Gray what I said—without any delay."

"He won't do a thing, Mr. Ferguson."

"He's your kin and clan head, Violette. He has a sworn duty."

I shake my head. "He won't. He doesn't like who I am."

"Well, I like who you are just fine, young lady. But you *have* to tell him I gave you this information. Do I have your word on it?"

"Yes, sir."

"Okay, then." He rubs the back of his neck like it's starting to hurt. "Story goes, Dale shot your daddy on account of your mama and all."

A clammy chill grips me and holds on like a haint. "What... what do you mean?"

"As I reckon, this happened about six, seven years ago. I hear tell Mrs. Woodbine, Hazel, that was her name, Hazel, and your maw were good friends. You know, did things together, like ladies do. But something bad happened with their friendship and that Blaylock church or maybe it was something that happened *at* the church. Not sure which it was. Your mama—and maybe Mrs. Woodbine, though I don't know that—left the church real quick. It would have been a much bigger... to-do, I suppose you'd call it, but that preacher kept the lid on, if I recall it correct." He shakes his head. "I'm not much for scandal-mongering."

"No, sir."

He keeps that stare on me, hikes up his work pants, and takes in a big breath. I can tell he's stalling for time and hates to say what's coming next, so I get ready best I can.

"Tale goes, the Woodbines, most likely Dale, went gunning for your mama after whatever it was that happened. Word has it Hazel Woodbine pleaded with her menfolks not to kill her. Well, they spared her life but killed your daddy instead. Made it look like an accident, right on Thanksgiving afternoon when all the men around here were deer hunting like we always do. And with the whole Woodbine clan in Sheriff Fletcher's pocket... well, nobody was brought to justice."

Dizzy and sick to my stomach, I lean against one of the rusted farm relics. "So, the Woodbines killed my daddy on account of my mama?"

He doesn't answer.

"And what was wrong with my mama and Mrs. Woodbine being friends?"

Mr. Ferguson looks away. "I couldn't say."

Does he mean couldn't or wouldn't?

Doc's footfalls crunch in the gravel, telling me my conversation with Mr. Ferguson is over. I walk behind Doc and Mr. Ferguson, trying to make my thoughts stop spinning. In the barn, I nod and pretend to be interested in Barley's colic when Doc talks about broad-spectrum antibiotic for him. But my mind is full to running over with Mr. Ferguson's words, the ones that came out of his mouth so easy and maybe changed my life forever.

16

"WELL," DOC SAYS, AS WE drive away from the Ferguson farm. "You did a good job out here. If you keep those grades up, and I know you will, I'm certain you'll make it into vet school. Also, where you live doesn't hurt. University admission people want some students from poor areas and give scholarships. That makes their stats look rounded out, which keeps their accrediting boards happy." She looks across at me. "What's wrong? Please don't think I'm trying to force vet school on you."

"No, it's not that. I want to be a vet more than anything in the world. But Mr. Ferguson, when I asked him... he practically told me *why* my daddy was killed and other stuff about my mama."

"What?"

"He said one of the Woodbines did it, probably Dale, which everybody thinks. But there was some kind of big trouble between my mama and Dale's. Mrs. Woodbine pleaded with her menfolk not to kill Mama, so they shot my daddy instead; made it look like an accident."

"That makes no sense, Vi. Unless… was there a feud between your clan and the Woodbines?"

"I don't know. I asked Mama, but she wouldn't tell me a thing."

"Let me think. You said your father died about seven years ago?"

"That's right."

"At that time, I was a new vet, fresh out of school and starting my practice in Blaylock. I didn't open the Bucktown office until a few years later. I'm trying to recall any talk in those days."

"That's okay," I say. "You were busy."

"No, there's something in the back of my mind, if only I could remember." She shakes her head. "I'll give it some thought."

When we drive into the clinic parking lot, it's filled with cars. "Wish I could stay and help you out. You have a full house, Doc."

"I appreciate that, but the best thing you can do for me is to go home, rest, and come back to work all well."

"Can I take a look at the puppy again?"

Doc swings her truck door open. "Of course."

We tread softly into the Trauma Room. "Look, Doc. She's worked herself partly out of the blanket." The dog raises her head a tiny bit and twitches her ears. "What do you think? At least she's more active."

"That's a super good sign. If she keeps responding this positively, I'll be one happy veterinarian."

I put my hand next to the pup's nose. "You keep getting better, Victory."

"Great name, Vi; so appropriate."

"Thanks. It just seemed right after what she's gone through. I mean, even living *this* long…

She smiles and nods. "Now. Home. Rest. Doctor's orders."

"Gotcha. On my way."

When I hoist myself into the truck, the pain in my side almost steals my breath, but it lets up a little on the drive home. I walk in the door, and a nail parlor smell blasts my nose. "Jess?"

"In here. Look. Whaddya think?" She waves half-painted emerald-green toenails at me.

"Glorious," I tell her with a grin. "The word is glorious."

She giggles. "I like it too."

"Jess, I gotta tell you something real… really important. Mr. Ferguson told me."

It must have been the tone of my voice, because her hand stops in midair and a splat of shiny emerald paint lands on her bare leg. "What?" she says, reaching for a cotton ball and polish remover.

"Where's Mama? Still in the garden?"

"Naw. She's making brownies for the church ladies."

I close our bedroom door. "It's about Mama and Mrs. Woodbine. Appears they used to be good friends, then something happened, like a big falling-out. Maybe that's what's in Dale's craw. He thinks our mama ruined their friendship, so he killed Daddy."

"Vi, that's the craziest thing I ever heard. Friends fall out all the time over nothing, except sometimes because of guys. Who is this Mr. Ferguson, anyway?"

"His farm animals are Doc's patients. He's awful nice, and I believe him."

Jessie shakes her head. "Well, don't believe him on this one; sounds like some put-up story to me."

"Yeah, but what if it *is* true? That could be why Dale's after us now. First, he kills Daddy, now all of us."

"So why would he let seven years go by and then decide to take the rest of us out? Makes no sense, Vi."

"Not unless Mama's done some harm to any of those Woodbines. I think we *gotta* talk to Uncle Gray. Don't see another way around it, do you?"

Jess blows blonde hair out of her eyes. "Not really. But let's hit up Mama first." She leads us down the hall, toenails half polished. "Hey, Mama. You got a minute?"

"What do y'all want? I'm trying to get brownies made for my prayer lunch tomorrow."

"Mama, Vi's learned some stuff we need to talk about."

"Why're you carrying on? I got no time—"

Jess puts her hand out. "No. You gotta make time. The brownies can wait."

"Well, get on with it. I'm already late with these."

"THAT'S THE BIGGEST PAIL OF hog slop I ever heard," Mama snarls, holding her wooden spoon over the brownie mix.

I watch chocolate batter drip off the spoon into the bowl and wait for her to say something, anything, that could help us. Can't help notice that her face is paler by a couple of shades and glistens with a sheen of sweat.

Jess and me, we stare at her and say nothing else. Finally, she clunks the ancient blue crockery bowl on the scarred counter and glares at us. "That Ferguson should shut his trap, making trouble like this for others. I'm gonna sic Gray on him. Why, he'll whip the tar out of that pissant."

I make my eyes small, and mean, and cold, like Dale's. "No Mama, you're not doing any such thing."

"Y'all don't know me. I can do any damn thing I put my mind to."

I step closer to Mama. "This isn't getting us anywhere. What happened between you and Mrs. Woodbine to put such terrible danger on us? We need to know—now."

She backs away from me like I've got lice. "I am fixing to tell you two nothing, because there's nothing to tell. Your daddy was killed in an accident, plain and simple; says so right on his death certificate. As for the Woodbines, I don't want to hear any of their names mentioned again in my house, hear?"

"Yes, we hear, Mama, and *you* need to know something too. Jess and me? We'll get to the truth of this mess, then take care of it ourselves."

UNCLE GRAY AND AUNT ZINNIE live in what she calls their ancestral home. Never one to be uppity, it's all the funnier that she says it. It's true the house has been on Sinclair land since forever, but it's not my idea of an ancestral home.

Their place isn't in the hollows like ours but almost at the top of Sinclair Mountain, one of the smallest in these parts but beautiful, with pine forests, and persimmon groves, and winter-blooming witch hazel trees scattered here and there.

With no moon, it's darker than a raven's eye at midnight as I make my way up the mountain. I take the switchbacks with a cupful of caution like Great Granny Sinclair says. When I pull up their driveway and park, my aunt opens the door before I can knock. "Hey there, child. Come on in and set down."

"Hey, Aunt Zinnie." Following her through the front room to the kitchen, I glance around the tidy house with its polished furniture. If it didn't stink so bad from cigarettes, this place would be perfect. "Where's Uncle Gray?"

"He'll be in directly after he tends to the chickens. We heard a coyote howlin' out back." Aunt Zinnie takes a long drag on her cigarette and fans smoke away from her face and mine. "Set down here at the table, Violette. So what's on your mind?"

Aunt Zinnie, bless her heart, always cuts right to the chase. "Uh, thought I'd wait for..."

The back screen door slams, and booted footfalls clomp down the hall.

"Here he is now, sugar." My aunt glances at me with what I'd call concern in her eyes, and I hope Uncle Gray's not in a foul mood. She crushes her cigarette butt in the ashtray, then lights a new one. "Look who's here to visit, Gray."

Uncle Gray, he's lanky and probably thin as he was at twenty. A deep crease channels down each cheek, and his face is more weather-beaten than any I've ever seen. He puts a look on me that doesn't include a smile. "Violette. How's your mama and sister?"

"They're okay, I suppose. How're you doing?"

"Oh, I'm doing, girl. I'm doing, if I can keep those damned varmints from my chickens."

"Yeah, Aunt Zinnie told me about that. Uh, I need to talk to the both of you about Mama and Jessie—and me too."

"You fixing to get yourself into more trouble? I heard about the last mess you got yourself into. Beat up and all."

I must have a startled look on my face because my uncle says, "You know how fast news travels 'round these hills, girl." He looks away from me and studies Aunt Zinnie's grease canister over on the stove, like he's never set eyes on it till now. "I shoulda come seen how you was doing, and I'm sorry I didn't. But you have to stay away from certain folks, Violette. Ain't you learned that yet?"

Wishing real hard I was out of here, I squeeze my hands together under the table and plow on. "Uncle Gray, there's things in this family... things that are causing harm, not only to me but Mama and Jessie too. And I need to know about them, so I can protect us."

Aunt Zinnie stubs out another just-lit cigarette and mashes it in the ashtray with about a million others. A tendril of blue smoke rises, and curls, then disappears, leaving the scent of secondhand tobacco. "Child, what *is* your problem? Is it more of this gay business? Because if it is, you got to get over it if you want to stay around here, like I said before you got beat up."

"No. Please listen to me. This is way past being gay or not. Can I tell you what I've come to tell you—and ask you?"

My uncle furrows his brow and rubs his rough hands together. "Go ahead, Violette. Your aunt and me, we'll listen, but there's no guarantee you'll like what we have to say when you finish."

"It's like this," I say. "Dale Woodbine's always been mean to me, but a few weeks ago he started threatening to kill me, and now he's after Mama and even Jessie. I need the connection between our mamas, because Dale said he wants... revenge for something Mama did to her. You know my mama; she probably insulted Mrs. Woodbine or something like that. I *gotta* find out to protect us. Can y'all help me?"

Uncle Gray blows out a big breath. "You need to talk to your mama about that one, Violette."

"I told her the same thing couple weeks back, Gray," my aunt says.

I look from one to the other before starting again. "I... I went to the sheriff, but he refused to help; acted like he didn't even know the Sinclair name. Said Dale's threatening me was a 'he said, she said' thing, and he couldn't help."

"It sounds like that rat's ass," Aunt Zinnie says, lighting another cigarette.

"So… only thing I can do is to catch Dale doing something illegal, like the dogfights or cooking. You know, something that'll send him to Jeff City for a long time. Junior agrees with me."

Uncle Gray rubs his right eye, and I bet it doesn't itch at all. "Violette, that's the most half-baked notion I ever heard. How in God's name you gonna do that? And what's Junior gonna do? Tackle him? Cart him off to the hoosegow?"

Aunt Zinnie stubs out her half-smoked cigarette, then adds it to her ashtray collection, and Uncle Gray slouches deeper in his old recliner. "That all, child?" she asks.

"Well, there *is* one more thing, and it goes along with Dale's threat. Uh, when I was out at Mr. Ferguson's farm? On vet business? I know him from the clinic. I asked him to tell me; he didn't want to. And before he did—tell me, that is—he made me promise to tell you, Uncle Gray, about what he was about to say."

I'm not explaining this good, by the confused looks on my uncle and aunt's faces.

"What, Violette? What the hell you talking about?"

"He… he said Daddy was shot because of something about Mama and Dale's mama. He didn't know—"

Uncle Gray slams his hand on the arm of his recliner. "Damn it, Violette. I heard enough of this garbage to last a lifetime. You're messing with things you got no place poking around in. Why're you doing this? Trying to ruin your daddy's *and* mama's reputation, are you? You know folks hereabouts got no money, no fancy education, nothing. All they have's their reputation, and you best not be diddling with that, or you'll be mightily sorry."

"But, Uncle Gray, we've been threatened, and I didn't start any of it."

"Like hell you didn't. Gallivanting all over creation, saying you're gay or whatever word you call it these days. As head of this clan, I can't protect you, Violette. God help me, I can't, seeing you've tied my hands. We defend our own under threats of death, but I can't do it if you won't follow clan rules. One of them's about men and women; their place in life and all. You know. Natural things."

Uncle Gray focuses on the edge of my left eye. "Besides that, there's things best forgot, left dead and buried for the ages. And it ain't your place to go digging them up for folks to see and sniff out. That's all I'm fixing to say."

My uncle quits talking, looks at his wife's cigarette, puts a hand out for it and takes a drag. I never saw him smoke until this moment, and it puts a chill on me, almost the likes I've never known. The recliner creaks and complains as Uncle Gray stands up. He stares at me, kind of uneasy, then shoves a kitchen chair tighter under the table, making a *thunking* sound as wood hits wood. Turning his back on me and Aunt Zinnie, he leaves the kitchen the way he came in.

My aunt's eyes hold worry when she finally looks at me. "Child, your daddy and Gray was close, as close as any brothers could be. Your daddy, he was the baby, and Gray, he always watched out for him his whole life, until the accident. Why, Gray was standing next to your daddy when he took the first shot."

"The *first* shot. How many times was Daddy shot?"

"I don't quite recollect, Violette, but that's no matter now. What *does* matter is he's dead and gone, and no amount of bringing up stuff from the past is gonna bring him back. What it *will* do is heap hurt on the Sinclair clan, mainly on you, and that's what your uncle's trying to keep from happening."

"But can't you see that I'm working to unravel a mystery here to keep Mama, and Jess, and me safe?"

"Violette, the things that'll keep you safest is, you go on home, keep your mouth shut, graduate high school, and settle down with some fella from these hills. There's nothing like a husband's protection, especially in these parts."

An attitude shifts between me and my aunt soon as she mentions settling down with a guy. She has rejected everything I've told her about my life. I know it, and she knows that I know it. Even with us not saying a word more, everything's forced and too polite. Aunt Zinnie, she won't look me in the eye either, and that's about the saddest thing that's happened tonight.

I stand up from the table where I ate so many meals, laughed so many laughs, and felt mostly at ease about myself. And where I probably won't eat another one or feel at home again. "Thank you for listening to me; appreciate it."

"Uh, y'all don't be a stranger now, sugar. Your uncle and me, we miss seeing you; seems like no time ago you was just little, and here you are all grown."

"Yeah. I guess that happens. Good night now."

I step outside, and my aunt shuts the door with a small click. I'm finished here and know it sure as I heard that coyote call across the mountain a minute ago. I stand by my truck and let memories of this place flow through me. As a kid, I loved being up here: a magic world, filled with mystery, and dark woods, and stories of ghost moonshiners. I hear an owl hoot nearby and can almost feel its wings flutter in the darkness. On this mountain, in this spot, is the only place in these Ozarks I'd be happy to call home.

I climb into the truck, and my mind overflows with memories made painful from my daddy's murder and a betrayal by those still alive. But snaking around them like smoke are happy ones too: Jess and me as little kids playing in these woods; Mama and Aunt Zinnie laughing and gossiping like the young women they were; and safety, everywhere safety, before I started to grow up into the scared and pitiful person I am today. I try to prize the images out of my head, so plaintive and painful they are to think on.

If Uncle Gray won't help us Sinclairs with Dale or the sheriff, then *I* will. Getting respect back for our clan will fall to me, the girl my uncle says made it disappear. I'll make it happen somehow, right along with what I've got to do for Jessie, and Mama, and me.

Turning around in their driveway, I look both ways, then ease onto the corkscrew road. After the fourth switchback, I hear a motor rev up where none should be. In seconds, a vehicle is inches behind me. Its driver blasts its high beams, then flips on a row of spotlights all along the top. He's blinding me! I flip my rearview mirror into the dark position, but even that doesn't help. *Don't spin out on the gravel. I have to hold it steady or pitch over this mountain.* Then I get it. Somebody's *trying* to pitch me over the mountain, trying to kill me and make it look like an accident. Folks die on these roads a lot more than they should, so no one would even be suspicious.

Within seconds, my truck is butted and slammed into the tiny guardrail with a sickening shudder. The monster truck jerks into reverse and backs up the narrow road. He's gonna plow into me again!

I shift into reverse and steer into the center of the road. Bracing my body, I wait for a gunshot to shatter the back window, while I mash the gear into first. No gunshot, so I sneak one look back, just one. The truck hasn't moved. But I do; right on down the mountain, hightailing it like I got Satan sniffing at my wheels.

Who the hell's driving that beast? For sure it ain't Dale. No way could he afford it. Unless he's had a payoff from the fights, which haven't happened yet, at least not in these hills. No, has to be Rucker. He's into bank robbery; said so, big as life on that *Missouri's Most Wanted* sign at the sheriff's office.

I shiver and look in the rearview mirror again. It reveals nothing but darkness.

ALL THE WAY HOME MY eyes dart between road and rearview mirror. I turn the truck onto Hollows Road with its familiar ruts and ridges and start to feel a tad safe. I park behind Mama, slide out of the seat and pretty near fly to the front door. Fumbling with my key, I drop the bunch. *Damn! Calm down. Get it in the lock.* Once inside, I bang the deadbolt home. My legs buckle, and my butt takes the fall with a soft thud. Terror and safety wash over me. Terror wins.

Jessie. I need to see her. *Damn.* She's sleeping over at Jewel's. Mama must be in bed, with the house so quiet; only sound's the clock ticking here in the front room. *Check the back door!* I cat-tread across the old kitchen floorboards, and then my heart nearly gives out. *What's that light coming from under the cellar door?* Mama probably took some of her just put-up garden vegetables down earlier and forgot to turn off the light.

I open the door and pray it doesn't creak. The stairs are black as pine pitch, so the light has to be on over Mama's shelf area. A sound, guttural and ghostly, floats on the air. Hair raises on the back of my neck, and an icy chill crawls up my back. What is it? An animal. No, an animal couldn't turn on the light. Maybe Mama forgot to turn it off, and then an animal got in. *Enough of this dilly-dallying. Go down those steps, and see what's there.*

Still as a grave. That's how I tiptoe down, gripping the rail to keep from bounding back up. When I reach the shadowy bottom step, my breath catches, and I slam my hand against my mouth to keep from screaming. A figure's hunkered on the wooden bench, all stooped over like a haint from the deepest woods. With its back toward me, the overhead light casts a giant twin on the wall. *How long has this house been haunted?*

Strewn all over the floor are envelopes, too many to count. When the haint starts sobbing and moaning over a piece of paper in its hand, I nearly collapse and grab the handrail again. *Sweet Jesus. It's Mama!* While she rocks back and forth, I stand there, knees shaking. What the hell's happening here? I remind myself it's Mama, not a haint, and maybe she needs me. I step quiet as a cat toward her, then stop. I . . . I don't know what to do. Pitiful as it is, I don't rightly know her enough to give comfort.

My feet falter and I stumble and almost fall. *Did she see me?* No worries about that. Mama's someplace else, surely not in this cellar. I retrace my steps to the bottom stair, never turning away from her. Slow as molasses on snow, I tread backwards up each step, praying it won't creak. When I reach the top, I stop and listen again. Nothing but the same terrible wails fill the cellar. Only after closing the door do I remember to breathe.

*   *   *

A DIRTY LIGHT FILTERS THROUGH our window, and I squint at my clock. Six forty-two. Sitting up, I realize I'm still dressed except for my black flip-flops, and memories from last night flood my mind. What in God's name did I see in that cellar? I shudder deep in my bones and throw off the comforter Grandma Sinclair made for me so many years ago. Gotta get outside and clear my head of clutter, so maybe I can think straight.

I'm put in mind of that Miss Havisham in the Charles Dickens book we had to read last year; that one about the bride who was jilted on her wedding day, then shut herself away for life. I tiptoe to the front room and open the door. When a moist breeze fans my face, Miss Havisham evaporates from my mind and floats back into the book I can't name.

Sinclair Woods, across from our house, is quiet and dark. Only now it looks dangerous too. A terrible understanding shoots through my body. I'm lucky to be alive after that mountain incident. Whoever it was must have wanted to kill me *real* bad. Folks around here have a good reason to fear Grayson Sinclair. So, to drive anywhere on his property, including that road? They're asking for an early grave.

A bird calls from somewhere deep in the woodlands, and another one closer to me answers. I stare at the woods and think about what it would be like to die. "What's this day gonna bring?" I whisper. "Good Lord only knows."

A rattling clatter from down our gravel road drags me away from last night's terror. Jewel's driving Jessie home in her calamity of a car. It lurches up to Mama's back bumper, missing it by about an inch. I wave to the girls. "You two are out early this morning."

Jewel leans her arm on the open window. "Oh, uh, I got some business up Hog Back today. I need to get going."

My heart gives me an unwanted thump. "Hog Back? You be real careful up there."

She squints too-made-up eyes, tosses long black hair over one shoulder, and turns her pouty blood-red lips down at the corners. "I can handle myself, Vi."

"Hope so. It can be rough up there for a girl your age."

Jewel puts a disgusted look on me. She shifts the car into reverse, noses it on toward town, and then rumbles off down the road.

Me and my sister, we stand side by side, staring after Jewel till the car is out of sight. "So what's going on?" Jess says, giving me a frown. "You look like hell."

"Well, good morning to you, Jessie."

"Aw, come on. You know what I mean."

"Yeah, I do, and there's a reason," I say. "Let's sit on the porch. Mama hasn't opened the kitchen window yet, so we can talk private."

Jess shrugs, letting me know talking about troubles is the last thing she wants to do this morning. She plops down on the top step across from me and crosses her legs. "So, shoot. What's the reason you look like the walking dead."

I'm leaving Mama and the cellar till last.

JESS LISTENS WHILE I GO on about Aunt Zinnie and Uncle Gray and me almost getting killed on Sinclair Mountain Road. She twirls her yellow ponytail, and pops blue bubbles, and scrunches her face a lot. But she doesn't interrupt. Not once.

Jessie uncrosses her legs, pulls her knees up to her chin, and wraps her arms around them. "This is real serious, Vi. Worse than I thought in the beginning. You told Junior?"

"No, not yet, but I'm gonna call him today."

"You need to right quick. He... I was wrong about him. He's got your best interests at heart. If you weren't, I mean..." Jessie lowers her eyes, realizing she's in uncomfortable territory, if I know her.

"I get it, sis. I've thought about Junior and me before. And I'm pretty sure he has too. I wish... no, I don't wish. It would be... convenient but it wouldn't work, wouldn't be fair to him or to me in any way."

"Yeah."

"Jessie, I..."

"What, Vi? I won't think bad of you; not anymore, not ever again. Even when we have fights... which I know we will... they won't be about your... sexuality."

I smile inside; she's trying out a new term, and I love her for it. "I know, Jess. It's just that since we're talking about Junior and all... I need... want to tell you something."

Her whole body gets quiet, like she's turned into one of those Greek mythology statues we studied a couple of years back.

I look her in the eyes, then stare off toward Sinclair Woods. "I... I've tried to like guys that way, mainly so I can fit in, be part of things. And I've tried to be like you, all girly, thinking that'd take away my troubles. But none of it worked, because deep down in my heart where it counts, I know. There wasn't a time I didn't know, or couldn't remember, not liking girls."

Jessie stares at me, unblinking.

"In my seventeen years, I never once kissed a girl in a romantic way except for Brandy Nesbit at school when we got caught, so that didn't count. I never made out in the backseat of a car, or even wrote a love letter to a girl that actually got delivered. Not once, not ever, Jess. I wish so bad for those things to happen, and I have my dreams, but most likely they'll be a long time coming. Living around here, anyway."

Jessie runs her hand over the porch step like she's smoothing out wrinkles on the ironing board. "It means so much...that you'd share those thoughts with me. I'm sorry I never, like... even knew who you were till I thought *I* was in a bad jam; that sounds, it was... so selfish."

I shrug. "Don't worry. I've wanted you to know for a long time; never knew how to tell you, and for so long we, well, you know..."

Jessie and me, we take each other's hand across the rotten part of the top step and sit quiet. Not much else needs saying.

"Listen, Jess," I say after a minute or so. "I have to tell you something important about Mama that I saw last night." I glance at the kitchen window, making sure it's still shut tight.

She wrinkles up her face. "Now, what?"

"It's kind of shocking, so get ready."

"Tell me."

"IT'S MR. WOODBINE OR ONE of his kin writing to her," Jessie says, like she knows it for sure, after I finish the story. "They're love letters. And that's why Mrs. Woodbine got so worked up over Mama. You see? It *was* about a guy, like I said." She celebrates being right by pushing her hair behind her ears. "*Now* it makes sense."

"Well, maybe you're right, Jess. You should have been there. You would *not* have believed it. Heck, I'm still having a hard time, and I *saw* the whole thing."

Jessie has this kind of faraway look in her eyes like she's trying to see our mama bellowing in the cellar. "Should we look for the letters or whatever they were?"

"Don't know yet; what's right to do. I... We need to think on it and decide later."

Jessie's phone rings, and she pulls it out of her pocket. "It's Jewel. I'll call her back later."

"So, you have fun at your sleepover last night?"

Jessie wrinkles her nose. "Ye-ah, I did."

"Doesn't sound like you're so sure."

"No, no, it was okay, only... Jewel, all she does is talk about sex and how she's doing it with a *couple* of guys."

"Well, that's pretty dumb, if you ask me." I smile. "Course, you're not asking me, are you?"

She shakes her head. "I guess not, but Jewel, she needs to be careful, but she won't listen to me these days." Jess tucks her phone back into her shorts pocket then pats it. "One of them's from Blaylock. That Declan Forsyth kid. He helps his daddy run a huge still over by Hog Back. You know that place everybody can smell? He's gotta be paying off the law, 'cause they make tons more than the government allows a family to brew for themselves."

"Probably."

"But anyway, this other guy she talks about? He's a criminal. A robber or something and all mixed up in that dogfight ring that's supposed to be coming too."

I shiver down to my toenails. "Well, that's downright dangerous for Jewel. Who is he, anyway?"

Jessie shrugs. "All's I know is she calls him Rucker the f—" She looks at me quick-like, then keeps on talking. "Jewel, she says the most fun is going up Hog Back with this guy in some old tent. I don't know. Sounds like a lot of work for what you get to me."

I'm pretty sure my ears can't be working.

"Vi? You okay? You look like you're seeing one of Grandma's ghosts."

"Let me tell you about Rucker, Jess. But if you think I'm in danger now, you tell anyone, especially Jewel? You're looking right into a dead girl's eyes."

19

SOMETIMES OF A SATURDAY MORNING, Mama makes Granny
Ross's buttermilk biscuits, and we eat them with her put-up jam.
My nose picks up a trace of that amazing smell when my phone
rings right after dawn.

"Hey, Vi." Junior says. "I'll take you up Hog Back today if you
want to look more for the dogfight place."

"You will? Why the change of heart, Junie?"

"'Cause you'll go alone, if I know you. That's why. And with
what you told me yesterday about what happened night before last
on Sinclair Mountain Road? I reckon we gotta stop just carrying on
about Dale, and Rucker, and the fights. We either back off totally
or go for it. Let's decide which it's gonna be, once and for all."

"Well, I'm for having another look-see now you mention it, but
driving up there hasn't crossed my mind anymore," I totally lie.

"Yeah, sure. Pick you up in about an hour. Okay by you?"

"Great. See you soon," I say and head for the kitchen.

"Hey, Vi," Jessie says, her mouth stuffed with biscuit and
raspberry jam.

I snag a steaming biscuit off the platter, the one that has only an outline of flowers from years of washing. "Best biscuits in Hitchens County, Mama."

Jess licks jam from around the edges of another biscuit, reminding me of when she was a little girl. "Mmm. So good. What're you doing today, Vi?"

"Well, Junior and me, we're taking a drive. You know. Just get away awhile, since we both don't have to work and all."

Mama opens her mouth, and Jessie's eyes go all wide. Time to get out now. "Okay, y'all. Gonna wait on the front porch. And, Mama? I appreciate the breakfast; it was awesome."

I open the front screen, and it bangs shut behind me. *Come on, Junie.*

I don't have to wait long. Truth to tell, he's fast as a frog hopping to keep his legs at suppertime.

Soon as his truck pulls up behind Mama's car, I make a dash to it. I open the door and slide in. "That was awesome fast, Junie. Let's get outta here before we get grumbling from Mama and Jessie. Silly them," I say with a grin. "They think we're going up Hog Back."

Junior raises his eyebrows at me but says nothing.

Most all the way up the mountain, the two of us are quiet. Must be the way soldiers feel, going into battle: not knowing what to expect, but it could be the worst.

At a rusted-out stop sign, Junior turns right onto the dusty road that leads to the meadow with the footpath. "Think you can remember where you found Victory?"

"Sure. It'll be in my mind forever." I point to the tiny lane slightly ahead of us. "Drive on in through those overhanging branches. Meadow's on our left."

Junior's truck slips under the canopy of small trees, knocking leaves off as we go. "How in the bejesus did you locate this place?"

"It looked suspicious, with all those tattered leaves hanging over everywhere. Uh, and it was about the only area I hadn't looked." I point to the right. "Here's where I parked last time."

Junior makes a turn into the field and parks. We scoot on out of the truck and lock the doors. "This heat sucks, and the bugs are worse, Junie. Should have worn jeans and boots. Probably thousands of ticks in tall grass like this."

"Aw, they're not so bad if you don't mind Lyme disease and Rocky Mountain spotted fever."

I give him a look. "Why Jewel would bare her bottom up here is a mystery to me with those eight-legged varmints everywhere."

Junior coughs, then pats his chest. "I don't know the answer, but you sure got a way of putting things."

I shrug. "Here's that sign warning people not to blab about what goes on in these parts. Over there's where I found Victory."

"One lucky dog."

"Lucky me, too. This is as far as I went last time, Junie."

"I'll go first," he says.

"Happy to oblige you on that."

I trudge along behind Junior, trying to step where he matted down the weeds. Less chance for ticks to jump on me. The August sun blazes overhead, and horseflies and gnats make walking a misery. "How long you think we've walked since that sign, Junie?"

"Not sure; maybe five, ten minutes, but we need to stop at the top of this ravine and listen before going on."

I'm grateful for this short break and wipe my face with my T-shirt tail.

"Don't hear a thing," Junior says after a few seconds.

We start down the slope when a tan blur flashes through the brush to my right.

"Drop, Vi!"

Oof. I hit the ground with Junie on top of me. Metal. I feel metal and realize he's packing.

"Couple of does. Scared 'em when we started walking. Let me give you a hand up, Vi."

"I've never seen you with a concealed gun. You must think we're gonna run into real trouble."

"Never know on Hog Back. Never know."

I run my fingers through my hair. Never know about ticks, either. "Boy, you move fast when you have to."

"Football," he says, looking left and right constantly until we make it to the top of the ravine.

"Hey, Junie, that little meadow laying beyond the patch of woods ahead of us? I see a beat-up old barn."

"Could be it, with that sign so close back there. Most country folk have these dogfights in a pit they dug out or an old barn."

"It's totally dilapidated," I say. "Can't be safe. Also, if this *is* the place, finding it was too easy."

Junior cracks his knuckles. "Yeah, but like I said, this *could* be it. And if it is, we gotta be careful walking out in the open, especially since old Rucker's supposed to have a tent somewhere round here."

My heart kicks into high gear. I'm not as brave as I'm putting on. "Uh, maybe we should keep a watch on that barn a few minutes, then go on over."

"I'm okay with that." He plops down under an oak tree.

"How can you sit on the ground out here in these woods, Junie? I'm not about to put my legs or butt anywhere near where ticks can fall or prowl around on me."

"What're you gonna do about that phobia when you're a vet? Those farm animals are full of them."

"Don't know. I gotta get over it, only not right now."

I FORCE MY EYES TO scan the landscape for anything different: manmade or odd. Funny thing is the peace and quiet of this place, even with danger always lurking on Hog Back. Only movement is a breeze blowing a few leaves in the stand of wild dogwood trees ahead of us. Red berries will appear in a few weeks, and in the spring these small trees will be covered in white blossoms, looking for all the world like their branches are snow-covered.

Junior whispers soft as he can in his loud voice, "Look over at the barn; three guys coming out. Something's going down." He cracks more knuckles. "They're almost too far away to tell anything. You know, like their ages or who they are."

"I don't think Rucker's one of them."

"Me neither," he says. "Looks like they're taking stock around the place, like maybe they're going to sell it, or tear it down, or look at a horse inside. Or get it ready for a dogfight.

Whatever, Vi, we need to investigate."

"Yeah, but how can we tell if they're gone or not?"

"Don't rightly know. We can't traipse around the barn. No cover. Maybe we listen for a truck motor to start. Only thing I can think of."

"But what if one of them stays at the barn or goes around it while the others leave?"

Junior rubs the top of his head. "Look, I got an idea. I'll go up first and do some snooping. If somebody's still there, I'll tell 'em I'm scoping out a good hunting place for the fall. People do that all the time."

"Yeah, that's good. They'd buy it."

"Okay, no better time than the present." He springs to his feet and wipes leaves off his jeans.

Tall clumps of wild grasses sway in the slight breeze, and thistles splash purple here and there, bobbing their heads as Junior weaves by them. The meadow's so beautiful. I wish I could enjoy it, but not with Junie out in the open. Not when he's at risk because of me. I gotta stop putting folks in life-and-death danger. Just can't think about it now.

Junior pauses, puts his hand to his forehead, and scans all over like he's looking for places where a deer might hide. He peeks around the far side of the barn, then walks back to the door and tries to open it. I can see that it won't budge.

My stomach sinks, and my palms are clammy. *Damn, it's locked. We should have thought of that.*

He disappears around the far corner of the building. *Be careful, Junie. Please be careful.* Please, no gunshots. Finally. He charges around the barn and looks in my direction. What's he doing, pushing his hands down, over and over, like he's exercising for football?

A slam of fear whacks my gut like a Dale punch. Someone's coming! I hit the ground, ticks or no ticks and push best as I can into some brush. Be invisible; think invisible. It's gotta be Rucker. Or Dale. I raise my head just enough to peer around. Over there. It *is* Rucker. He's not that many yards from me; other side of my brush cover. I scoot deeper into this thicket. Thorns. Gotta watch them. Don't dare move. Breeze isn't strong enough to tickle a mouse's whiskers in here.

Kachunk.

A rifle cocked! He's spotted me. My body almost rattles from the shakes; breath's all shallow. I wait for my insides to be torn apart. *Ka-boom!* The smoky smell of gunpowder drifts down to my nose. *Don't move or breathe hard. At least I'm alive. Who's he shooting at?*

"Goddamn it to hell!" Rucker yells above me. "You stupid rabbit. Don't you know I need something on my table tonight, and it's supposed to be you? Now what am I goin' to do? I'm fixing to have company, and look what you gone and done."

This is the craziest person I ever met.

Silent. So still. No birds calling. *Don't move yet. Don't hardly breathe. Wait to hear birds. Wait.* Finally, one warbles a frail melody. Another answers. *Am I alone?* The space feels empty. I ease out and belly crawl around the brush. Nobody's here, because Rucker's headed straight to Junior! I whip out my phone and text Junie. No signal. Jamming my body into the bush again, I peek through spaces in the thicket to where I reckon Junior may be.

There he is. Thank God. He creeps out from behind the barn, looks around, and gestures for me to come there. Guess he's hoping I see him. *In your dreams, Junie.* But when I look at him again, he's waving like a madman. *Okay, but you better be right on this one.*

Leaving my safe thicket, I tread across the meadow, scared spitless. But it's as calm and quiet as a regular Ozark summer day, and nobody's shooting. Yet.

The second I reach Junie, he whispers hoarsely, "What took you so long, Vi? Didn't you see me waving?"

"Yeah, but didn't you hear a shot in the woods? Rucker tried to shoot his meal."

Junior gives me a blank look. "He must have walked right by me, only I was on the other side of the barn looking in. Thought I heard a shot from somewhere."

"Ye-ah. He shot right over my head at a rabbit and scared the bejesus out of me. But when he missed it, he went nuts. Yelled at the rabbit and said it should have let him shoot it for his supper. Hell, Junie, that dude's not right."

"Maybe he was in prison so long he'll talk to anything."

"I don't know about that—"

Junior puts out his hand to shush me. "Listen, Vi. This barn's used for dogfights. It's outfitted with everything those low-lives need for that show. The doors are locked tight, but you can see in through part of a window they missed in covering them up."

"But how'd you manage that with no light?"

"Idiots left one of those big covered lights shining right in the middle of what they use for a ring. Take a look. See those heavy chains?"

I don't want to hear this, but I look, anyway.

"They're used to weigh down young dogs so their front muscles will get super strong. And that collar made with inward spikes is used for cruelty to toughen them up. Jake told me about this stuff, but I never saw it before. Terrible."

"Look at that, Junie. It's like they tried to clean up the blood, but a lot's still there, soaked up by sawdust in the ring. C'mon. Let's get out of here. I'm near sick seeing this stuff, and not knowing Dale's location is making me real jumpy."

"Okay. I'll take the lead again," he says, and begins trekking across the meadow.

I follow him, whipping my head right and left so much, it almost leaves me dizzy.

A light breeze stirs the leaves of persimmon trees edging the woods. Tall pines stand behind them like guards, waiting for the soft orange fruit to fall in November.

Junie brings me back to brutal reality when he whispers, "Ravine's coming up ahead, so not much longer."

His boots crunch hickory nuts. Getting to be that time. If Mama was with us, she'd put us both to work gathering them for a hickory pie, her favorite. A pang pricks my heart. It was Daddy's too.

After crossing the ravine, we hike through the woods and pass by the place where I found Victory. At the barbed wire fence, I say, "There's your truck, Junie. Let's get to it fast."

"Boy, you *are* jumpy. Calm down. We're here."

I shiver. "My back's tingling like it's knows a slug's on the way. Maybe I'm a coward."

"You?" He gives me a look and unlocks the door.

I scoot in quick and lock the door.

Junie wipes his face on his T-shirt tail. "*Phew.* Hot in here. Lemme get the AC going."

Bam! Bam! Bam! Somebody pounds on the truck's side. "What the…" Junior lowers his window.

"Violette! Hey, Violette!" comes a familiar voice from behind us. "What're y'all doing up here?"

"Oh, my God. It's Jewel. What're we gonna do now?"

Junior half opens his door, looks over at me, and says real soft, "We'll figure it out as we go."

I step out of the truck onto thick pine needles. "Hey, Jewel. What're you doing up here?"

She stares at me hard. "I think I asked you first. Plus, how'd you find this place in the whole Ozarks?"

Junior puts his fists together and double-snaps his fingers like I can never do. "Aw, she's just up here with me, Jewel. Fall coming and all, I'm scoping out new places to deer hunt."

"Yeah, but y'all didn't answer my question. Why *this* place?"

He gives her an exasperated look. "C'mon. You know I've got cousins up here on Hog Back. I'm just refreshing my mind on good hunting grounds."

She scrunches up her face like she hates his answer. "What I don't get is why not hunt in Sinclair Woods? She lowers her eyes a second, then lays a hard stare on Junior. "I mean, you do everything with Violette except—"

Junie glares at her. "You're way out of line, Jewel, so shut your mouth."

She shuts it, but I can't shut mine. "You know well as anyone that nobody can hunt in those woods. Uncle Gray, he'd kill them if they weren't in the Sinclair clan. And they'd still have to get his permission."

Jewel scowls at me. "Well, you being Jessie's sister and her friend, I'll give y'all a good tip. It's best not to come back here to hunt or do… anything, if you know what's good for you."

I'm so pissed, I won't let it go. "What's the big deal about not hunting around here? We looked for *No Hunting* signs and didn't see any."

Jewel lifts the back of her hair and hand-fans her neck. "Take or leave my advice, but you both been warned, good and proper. That's all's I'm fixing to say." She turns with a girly flounce that puts me in mind of Jessie, sashays to the meadow trail, and is swallowed up by the woods.

Neither of us say a word until we turn off the cracked asphalt and onto the big two-laner heading down the mountain to Bucktown; back to where it's safe, or at least safer than Hog Back Mountain.

"Junie?"

"Yeah."

"I'm pretty sure you don't care to hear one more thing about my crazy family, but I gotta tell you something about Mama. See what you think. Okay?"

"Shoot," he says and gives me a quick glance. "Maybe that was a bad word choice."

JUNIOR LISTENS ALL QUIET UNTIL I finish. "It's a no-brainer, Vi. They're love letters from one of the Woodbine menfolk, probably Dale's paw. Has to be, from what you told me. I mean, her sitting around suffering like a lovesick mule—I'm not calling your maw a mule, mind you—but what else could it be?"

"Yeah, that's what Jessie said, too, but how about if something else terrible bad happened to her, Junie?"

"Like what?"

"Like something we're not thinking of."

"You gotta face that it's one of those Woodbine men, Vi. I mean, all those letters? That's why Mrs. Woodbine and your maw had such a falling out. Wouldn't be a thing else to cause that bad a ruckus."

I shrug. "You're probably right."

"You don't think so?"

I shrug again.

"Well, Vi, you tell me how something like that's *gonna* make a person feel. All jealous, and madder'n hell, that's how."

"I know. I just don't want to accept it."

"I... I'd feel the same about my maw, Vi, but our maws are women first and maws second."

I mess with his truck's passenger side air-conditioning vent, aiming it right at my face. Closing my eyes, I try to clear my mind. "I don't want to think about it anymore. What should we do next about Dale and all; that is, if you want to? I mean, you're putting yourself in awful danger. You want to have a think on it before carrying on?"

"I've *been* thinking on it. Seems to me you need help, a lot of help after what just happened up Hog Back." He looks hard over at me, and I know another reason's coming. "These are the kinds of guys Jake looks up to. If they can get some hard jail time, maybe he'll finally get what can happen and change his ways. Anyhow, that's what I'm counting on."

"Jake's lucky to have a brother like you. I hope he knows it."

Junior doesn't say anything to that because he hates compliments, but it's so, all the same. Instead, he says, "The way I figure is we need to shift the focus back on Dale again, find out if he's *definitely* part of this ring. Like you say, if we can prove that, we got him."

"But if we do get him," I say, "we gotta locate someone in the law who's not dishonest, doesn't have a stake in the fights, and wants to bring these no-accounts to justice."

"Only one problem I can see, Vi. That's gonna be a hell of a lot harder than getting through those pearly gates your maw believes in so much."

21

DOC FINISHES VICTORY'S REGULAR MORNING exam, sighs, and
gives me a look. "This pup's going to take a while longer to finish
her internal healing, but she can go home and do it. No more
IVs, her sutures are healing nicely, and she's getting much of her
strength back. I'm sorry about this timing, Vi, but she needs to be
freed right away. I'm sure this girl has spent much of her first year
caged up and should be out of one soon as she's able."

"I know," I say, "and you need the space too."

Doc places the stethoscope back around her neck. "Look, is
there anyone who can take care of her until we can arrange a home?
I'd love for her to be with you but, uh, also know the position
you're in there."

"I've been thinking hard on it. What... what about Mr.
Ferguson? He's so kind to animals. Think he'd take care of her for
a spell, until... if I can get things arranged with Mama?"

"It's worth a try. He thinks you're a very sincere young woman,
and you wanting to be a vet so badly has touched him. Would you
like me to call?"

"Yes. That would be great."

"I'll do it this morning and let you know."

"Thanks again, Doc," I say, yearning to be like her so much it hurts.

Victory paws at my hand as if she's telling me it's time for us to go now. "If you get to spend some time at Mr. Ferguson's farm, you'll love it there, girl." She gazes at me with her deep brown eyes. "And no matter what it takes, you and me are gonna be together. And you'll never be in a cage again." I throw that in for good measure and hope to sweet Jesus we can make it happen.

Later that day, as I drive back to the Bucktown Clinic, my phone rings. "Good news," Doc says. I just spoke with Mr. Ferguson, and he's happy to take the puppy for however long it takes; even said they'd adopt her if it comes to that, but only if you can't take her. He has to drop by this office to pick up vitamins for Barley, so he'll get her today."

"I'm beholden to you, Doc, and I'll try and get something worked out soon as possible."

"Take the time you need. Between him and me, we'll work it out."

SITTING HERE ON THE PORCH this afternoon with the washer beating our clothes to death and a couple mosquitoes humming around my face, I'm crazy worried about how to get Victory home.

Jessie drags up the porch steps from doing her cheerleading routine in the side yard. "Hotter than hell out here, you want my opinion. Got any more ideas about Mama and your dog?"

"No. You got any?"

"Not where Mama's concerned. You know what she's like when she makes up her mind, Vi."

I sigh and glance at Sinclair Woods. "Yeah, I—hey, what's that? Something shiny is reflecting over there. See it in the crook of that big white pine?"

"Yeah, I do. Probably nothing." She flops down on the edge of the porch and swings her legs over."

"You're likely to pick up a tick dragging your legs through that tall grass, Jessie."

"I swear. You and your ticks. You're driving me and everybody else nuts going on about them."

"I gotta get over it but don't know how. C'mon. Let's find out what's shining up there."

"Aw, Vi. It's nothing, and I'm still hotter than the devil dancing in hot grease."

"Well, I'm going and would sure appreciate you coming along."

She won't look me in the eye, but makes a big fuss out of fanning her face to let me know how scorched she is.

I cross the crunchy sunbaked grass and can't wait to step into the woods where everything is deep shade and smells of piney soil.

"Hold on. I'm coming," Jess yells from the porch.

"Great." I'm surprised how much better Jessie makes me feel by tagging along. These days you never know what can happen around here.

Afternoon shadows fill the woods, but here and there, shafts of sunlight carve up the dimness. Whatever I saw must have reflected off one of those beams. When twigs snap under my flip-flops, my eyes dart around, and I start to sweat, but not only from heat. About twelve feet ahead, something shiny is wedged in the crook of two branches of a huge white pine tree. I point to it. "There it is."

"Beer can, Vi. Silver. That has to be what was reflecting and all."

"Why up there?" I tiptoe around the tree trunk, and pretty near pass out. "Sweet Jesus, what's *this*?" It's a tree stand. But not for shooting deer. Not in Sinclair Woods. Not facing our house. Boards, new ones, have been nailed to the tree, making a rough ladder up to the crook.

"Hell's bells. What we got here?" My sister's voice is shaky, like I feel inside. She knows what it is too.

"I... I'm gonna go on up, Jess. Get a view of what they're trying to see or shoot."

I scan the area pretty good, hesitate a second, then climb on up the boards; six of them, each about two feet apart. Exactly what I thought. A straight line from tree to porch, a simple shot from a good marksman. Problem is that describes most everybody in these hills, since they live off the land and learn to shoot before first grade.

"What you see, Vi?" Jess yells up at me, soft as she can.

I've surely seen enough and scramble down the steps.

Jessie's still, real still, and I can tell she's waiting hard for my words.

"Uh, just what I thought. Somebody's got a bead right on the porch from this angle. They're planning to shoot us. Maybe not now, but they built that stand. They built it because they're coming back to use it. To help get a clean shot. A clean kill."

Jessie's eyes are dinner plates, and there's a wildness to them. Without a word, we tear out of the woods, across the yard, up the porch steps. Once inside, I throw the deadbolt behind us, the one Uncle Gray put on the day Daddy was shot. I feel sick to my stomach. I don't know how to fight this monster, Dale Woodbine.

Jessie is panting hard. "We *have* to tell the sheriff, Vi. He's gotta do something."

"He will *not* do a thing. There won't be fingerprints or footprints. Sure, the lumber's new, but everybody buys lumber at the yard all the time. Him even looking at it will prove nothing."

"Then let's ask Uncle Gray what to do. Let him worry with it. If he thinks anybody's hunting these woods, he'll have 'em for breakfast."

I make a scoffing sound. "Yeah, like he's helped us before. I went up there and practically begged him. You know he walked out on me. I won't ask him again. But I'm sure gonna tell Mama. Maybe it'll scare her into *finally* getting it that we're in life-and-death danger here. Then maybe she'll tell us what we need to know. And that might help us nail Dale and maybe Rucker."

"Don't count on it, Vi. I wouldn't count on it."

"Well, we got the reason to get Victory home now, Jess. I don't see how Mama can say no with that tree stand over there. Where is she, anyway?"

"Gone to Blaylock. Back late tonight after some kind of revival meeting."

"I can't ask her then. She'll be too worked up from all her church stuff. Have to wait till morning."

Jess nods. "She's always easier to talk to then, anyway."

22

I MASH OFF MY ALARM and roll over. To say I feel all done in wouldn't start to describe how tired I am. Much as I love my job, I'm awful glad to have the day off.

"Bad night again?" Jessie asks when I shuffle into the kitchen. She pours steaming coffee into one of our thick mugs. "You carried on in your sleep something fierce."

"That tree stand ran around in my head for hours. Sorry I disturbed you."

Jess gives a super-sized yawn. "Not a biggie. And good luck with Mama and getting Victory home."

"Oh, God. Gonna talk to her soon as I take my shower."

About fifteen minutes later, I traipse outside to the garden where Mama is every early morning in summer. Birds twitter, and yellow butterflies tend the flowers, and you could almost be fooled into believing it's a perfect life with no troubles to speak of. "Beautiful day, isn't it, Mama?"

"Not bad now, but it's gonna be a killer before nightfall, then we're in for a storm. Y'all better dress cool."

"I will, and I'll see to it that Jessie does too."

"Hmph," she says, letting me know my answer's satisfying to her.

"I need to talk to you about something important and I know you won't agree with me, but please listen."

"Violette, why do you always make trouble for this family?"

"Mama, hear me out first. Okay?"

Maybe it's because I talked nice to her; she puts the clippers in her garden basket and sits down on the step. "What is it now?"

"It's about Dale and a guy named Rucker Hicks. Do you know him?"

"I know of him. Why're you bringing him up? That fella, he's a bad sort, bad as they get. You want no truck with him."

"Exactly. And that's why we need a dog."

She starts to stand. "I'm telling you now, for the last time, no dog's coming into this house, peeing and bringing in fleas and dirt. No way, Violette."

"Just *listen* to me a minute longer. Let me tell you what's happened, because Rucker *is* involved. Jess and I found something… troubling over in the woods yesterday, and now I need to tell you the whole story."

She eases herself back onto the step. "Well, make it snappy. I don't have all day to listen to your farfetched reasons to bring a dog into my house."

SAME AS WITH JESSIE, MAMA doesn't interrupt one time when I tell her about finding Victory and the tree stand. But she gives me no answer when I finish talking. I'm quiet, then ask, "Did you hear what I said?"

She looks me in the eye but with no squint. "Violette, the deer stand, if that's what it is, could have been there for years."

"No, take a look at it. But don't go alone. It's brand-new wood; you can even smell how fresh it is. Dale for *sure* put it there, and these days, Rucker and him? Why, they're thick as the mud bottom in Cooter's Crick. Guaranteed they built that thing together."

Mama, she stares at me hard. "I gotta talk to Gray. And I'm telling him about you going back up that mountain after you got that summons or whatever it was. I know it was there you found that dog you want to bring in my house."

"No. Don't do that, at least, not right now. You know trouble can follow Uncle Gray, with his temper. All he'll do is... scare them off, make 'em clam up. Then they'll hit us when we're not looking 'cause they'll believe *we* think everything's okay. Junior and I have a plan."

"What kind of plan?"

"Better you don't know. For your own protection. You have to trust us, Mama."

"Violette—"

I put out my hand, hoping she'll let me talk. "Let's get Victory here to protect us. Then if things get worse, we bring Uncle Gray in. That work for you?"

Mama, she looks defeated, like I beat her down, or maybe it was the scary stuff I told her, but she doesn't say a word. Just stares at me.

"Gotta get to the clinic now. Thanks for listening."

"But I thought you didn't work today," Mama yells.

Pretending not to hear her, I dash out of the garden. Every smidge of tiredness has disappeared, and I sprint to the truck before she can yell back about not bringing Victory home.

Once I'm finished dodging the ruts on our road, I grab my phone and make the call I never thought would happen. "Hey, Mr. Ferguson," I say, after he picks up on the second ring.

"Hi, there, Violette. It's nice to hear your voice this morning. Your puppy's doing just great."

"Oh, thanks. I knew she would with you and Mrs. Ferguson. Uh, my mama said we could bring Victory home kind of unexpected, so I thought I should call and let you know."

"Well, we hate to say goodbye to her, but she'll be one happy pup. Will you be at the clinic today, Violette?"

"Yes, sir. I can be there any time."

"Well, that'll work out fine then, because I'm leaving now for the True Value in Blaylock, so I'll tote her over. "Will about half an hour be okay with you?"

"Sure. I'm in my truck now. See you then. Bye."

My insides are doing somersaults, and I can't stop grinning. Pulling off the road, I text Jess and Junior and hope the messages go through; these hills are a problem even trying to use a regular house telephone.

With about five minutes to spare, I drive too fast into the Blaylock Clinic parking lot, right next to Doc, who's climbing out of her truck. "Hey, Doc. I'm getting Victory now. Mama said it was okay."

She gives me a big smile. "Oh, wonderful. Is Mr. Ferguson bringing her here?"

"Yes, any minute now."

"That's just wonderful," she says again.

"For sure, Doc."

Before I can follow Doc inside, Mr. Ferguson's truck pulls into the parking lot. I can see Victory in the back seat, strapped into the seatbelt. "Good morning, Violette," he calls. "Somebody's waiting for you, and what a fine girl she is. You almost lost her to my wife, even after one night with us." He opens the door and unfastens the seatbelt. "I think a new puppy's in our future too."

"That'd be great."

"Now, Vi, she's one slippery wiggle," he says, setting her down light as possible.

I put my face close to hers and get about a zillion Victory kisses.

"She knows who saved her life, don't you, girl? This puppy's gonna be loyal to you her whole life, Violette. It's the special trait of a pit bull-terrier mix, like she is."

"I'm sure finding that out. Thank you for everything… for being so good to me and… for all of it."

"My pleasure. I'm happy to help you anytime, hear?"

"Yes, sir."

"And young'un, since I'm old enough to be your great-granddaddy, I'm going to give you some advice."

"Yes, sir," I say again.

"Okay, then. Here it is. Please don't go wandering around Hog Back anymore."

My face turns to fire, but Mr. Ferguson goes on with what he's saying. "Some real dangerous folks are up there, and no telling what they'd do to a pretty girl like you. I… have a hunch this has something to do with your daddy's death, but he wouldn't want you dead too."

"Thanks, Mr. Ferguson. I'll take what you said to heart, and—"

Doc opens the clinic door for us, and Victory starts her wiggle-dance all over. "Just look at you, almost as good as new. You're one lucky puppy." When Doc puts her hand down, palm close to Victory's face, she immediately sits.

"Wow. How'd you do that?"

"She's very teachable, Vi. She's so smart. I've got a couple training books that you can borrow. Just remind me."

"I sure will, and thanks to you both again, Doc and Mr. Ferguson. I wish I could repay you somehow. Maybe I'll think of a way."

"Don't go talking about payment, young lady. Seeing you and Victory well and happy is enough. Now, I'll get this girl strapped into her seatbelt. I'll put her in the front seat this one time to be closer to you; keep her anxiety down a mite."

"I'm obliged, Mr. Ferguson. And I hope to see you real soon."

Victory's calm on the way home. She glances at me pretty often, like she's saying, "Is this it? Are we going to my forever home?"

I can't wait to get there and show her that it is.

"Here they are, Mama," Jessie shouts so loud from the front porch that I can hear her from the truck.

"C'mon, puppy," I say. "Let's get you unbuckled. And put you down... real gentle." I use my leg muscles and not my back. My side gives a little twinge, but nothing I can't live with.

"Victory," Jessie calls, and the dog cocks her head and wags her tail. Jessie walks slowly up to her and holds out her hand.

"Look, she's doing the wiggle-dance for you, Jess. She likes you already."

Jessie squeals, "*Oooo!* She's so sweet!"

I grin at my sister and roll my eyes, code for *Now it's Mama's turn.*

"Well, let's see this dog of yours, Violette. Mighty beat-up, isn't it?"

"It's a she, Mama, and if you went through the kind of torment she's gone through in her short life, you'd be scarred too."

Mama puts a hard stare on the pup. "I reckon there's a bit of truth to that. Not gonna be any puppies to contend with, will there?"

"Nope. Doc fixed her, so no worries."

When Mama places her hand close to the dog's face, Victory takes a sniff and lowers her head.

I stop breathing.

But then she gives Mama a tiny hand lick. Then another. And one more. When I peek at Mama, she's smiling real big. Soon as she knows I'm watching, she shifts to her regular face. But it's too late, because I saw.

Jessie must have seen her smile too. "I didn't know you liked dogs."

"Well, Jessie, there's a lot you don't know about me."

I shake my head just a little bit. *Ain't that the truth?*

23

A SNARL WAKES ME UP. "Victory, you dreaming? Where are you, girl?" *First night here. She'll get used to the place.* Another snarl and a growl, this time near our window. A chill passes through me, and I sit up. Something—or someone's—out there, and she knows it.

I creep to the side of the window and peek through. Nothing but an almost-full moon casting long tree shadows on the grass. Nearby, a barn owl hoots. Victory presses against me. "Hey, girl." I stroke her head and neck; the head that's pressed against the screen, the neck with hackles as high as they can go. "What do you see out there?"

Bam! A shot blasts the night in half. *Bam! Bam!* "My God," Jessie screams. "Vi! Are you all right?"

"I... think so. Roll off your bed. Get flat on the floor."

The old wood creaks as Jess hits it. "Vi. Vi. You get down too."

The puppy is barking, and growling, and howling, and I can't get hold of her. "Victory. Quiet. Come here!" She's gonna rip through the screen, get herself shot.

Mama tears into our room, slams the door behind her, and stands against it like she's part of the wood. "You girls okay?"

"Yeah. Stay back," I whisper loudly.

Mama's breathing hard. "Think I'm safe here, Violette."

Panic sets hard on me. "I can't reach the dog. Quiet, Victory."

"We gotta get her away from the window, Vi. She's a clear target." Jess crawls over on her belly and snags the dog by her collar, then pulls her away from the windowsill and out of the room.

Bam! Another gunshot splits the night, this time shattering the plaster above Jessie's bed. "Oh, my God." I lunge for my phone on the chifforobe, crawl out of the room, and dial nine-one-one.

"Nine-one-one," the operator says after two rings. "What is your emergency?"

"Somebody's shooting at us, into our house, four shots so far."

"Where do you live, ma'am?"

"On Hollows Road, the Sinclair house."

"Are you alone?"

"No, my mama and sister are here too."

"Who am I speaking to?"

"Violette. Violette Sinclair. And could they hurry?"

"I've just dispatched a car. Should be there soon. Stay inside, keep low, and I'll be on the line."

"Thank you," I say, in the shakiest voice I've ever heard from me.

THE OFFICER CLOSES HIS NOTEBOOK. "Well, I think that's about it for now. I'm reckoning it could be bear or 'coon hunters. You know, those guys do their hunting at night."

I stare at him like I'm dealing with an idiot, which I pretty much am. "Bear hunters! You never see a bear around here, only in the higher mountains and then not much. As far as 'coons go, nobody'd shoot at a house to get one. That doesn't sound right to me."

"Oh, you'd be surprised."

"Sir, it's a full moon tonight. How could they not see a house?"

"Well, you know. Stray bullets. Happens all the time."

"Three of them? One directly over my sister's bed. Really?"

The officer finds a piece of invisible lint on his shirt interesting. "I seen things like that myself during hunting season."

"But I just told you what's been happening and about me talking to Sheriff Fletcher. You don't take that into account with this shooting?"

"Sure I do. But if the sheriff don't think there's anything to your story, it's good enough for me. Look, I told you I'll run it by him, and I will. But if you hear nothing back, well, then…"

My chest is hot, and I'm so frustrated, the spit's pretty well dried up in my mouth. "But it's *not* hunting season, and everything is worse than before. Can't you see that? What about the new tree stand aimed at our house? Shouldn't you check it out in daylight? You going to tell the sheriff about it?"

He says nothing, only fidgets with his notebook, the one where he didn't take down a single word. "Look, ladies. We get a lot of stray gunshots around here, and during the season, more hunters than you can shake a stick at. You must know that, living in these parts so long. As for that stand? No telling how many years that thing's been there. Why not ask your kin, Gray Sinclair about it? He'll tell you what I'm saying is the unvarnished truth."

"And Officer, if you know Gray Sinclair, then you also know he would shoot anyone other *than* kin for putting a tree stand in those woods. And even then they'd have to have a damn good reason, like starving."

"Look, Miss... Sinclair, is it?"

"Yes, for the second time. You know, niece of *Gray Sinclair*?"

"Oh, yeah. Uh, the perimeter's been searched, and I used my flashlight for footprints but didn't see any. Look, ladies. I know we got a full moon out there now, but heavy weather's brewing. Should be ugly by early morning, so finding any footprints is gonna be nigh impossible." He stands and tucks the notebook in a top pocket, then feels to be sure it's there. "Well, them's the breaks, I guess. Not a thing to be done about the weather."

I can't believe all he's going to do is exactly nothing. I want him to... I don't know what, but I surely wasn't expecting a bear alert or weather report.

*   *   *

MAMA SLAMS HER COFFEE MUG on the table, spilling steaming hot liquid onto the scarred wood. "This time you're not talking me out of calling Gray. I shoulda told him last night; had *him* talk to that dimwitted policeman." Her eyes contain such fire, I'm surprised they don't leave me scorched. "Look what you've gone and done, Violette. People trying to kill us everywhere we turn. Lord in Heaven, what did I do to deserve a daughter like you?"

I want to yell and scream and ask her if she has no recollection of why all this started. How I was threatened, and tormented, and beat to a pulp. But I don't, because it's no use.

"C'mon, Victory. Let's take a look around outside to see what's damaged."

I leave Mama sopping up the spilled coffee with her ratty sponge, lips pursed in a tight line.

When I open the back door and breathe in clammy air, I'm put in mind of visiting Merrimac Caverns in the foothills, the place where all the St. Louis tourists go for a day out, then spend the rest of it driving around, gawking at us country folks in the hopes we'll do or say something stupid.

Victory and me, we step outside, and a silver world swallows us up. Mist dampens my face, and a drop of water plops on the back of my neck, sending chilly shivers through me. The pup feels it too. She shakes real hard, and her fur ripples all down her back. At least that brainless officer got the weather right.

"Come on, girl. Gotta keep our eyes peeled. Probably still dangerous as hell out here." Traipsing around the house makes me shudder. Sinclair Woods looms ahead of me and a little to my right. This morning it has a brooding atmosphere, with low-slung fog swirling around tree trunks. It feels full of trolls, and witches, and haints. But what could be there waiting for me may be a lot worse than things conjured up in my head.

I scan the tree line for signs of anybody trying to hide. Shivering, I turn back to examine the house. "Would you look at that, Victory?" Directly under the eaves are three bullet holes almost in a triangle. My heart kicks me in the chest. These came straight from the woods, where we're easy pickings from that pine tree. From that stand. We're gonna get killed. And soon, if I can't figure out what to do.

The two of us tromp back around the house, shoes and paws sopping. "Let's dry off on the rag rug, girl, soon as I get this door locked up real tight."

"No, Mama," I hear Jessie say, when I pad into our bedroom. "It's only a small hole that we can fix ourselves." She rolls her eyes and hands me the bullet Mama dug out of the wall. "Isn't that right, Vi?"

I put it in my shorts pocket to save as evidence. "Yep. We can repair this wall good as new. Don't need to spend any money on it."

Jessie's face is drawn and pale. She looks like I feel.

"Uh, Mama," I say. "Maybe we *do* need to talk to Uncle Gray after what happened last night."

"You're right, Vi," Jessie says. "I know you and Junior are gonna be upset about your plan to nab Dale and all. But with finding that tree stand and now getting the house shot up? I mean, we're targets here."

My insides feel all hopeless, but I nod my head. "Mama, you need to be the one who calls Uncle Gray. He won't listen to me or Jess."

She wrings her hands. "Well, I always rely on Gray to fix things, but now that I'm pondering it through, this is different. Real different."

Jessie nods. "Yeah, it's different. Dangerous different. Give him a call, Mama."

"No, I mean Gray. He'll go and stir the pot, if I know him," Mama says, sort of talking to herself. "Folks will bring up old troubles; you know, gossip and such around these parts. Won't do nobody a lick of good, you ask me. To get Gray all het up, I mean."

"Then what do you want to do?" I ask her. "You *know* I didn't want to get Uncle Gray involved, but after this shooting, things have gone too far."

Mama, she stares at me hard. "What *about* that plan you're always goin' on about? The one you cooked up with Junior."

"Well, we need to get the goods on Dale and Rucker. Only way I can figure to do that is catch them in something illegal, like the dogfights. So Junior and me… Junior and I have been working on how to do it."

Mama frowns at me like I just told her I have the plague. "That's it? That's your plan?"

"Look—"

This time it's Mama who puts out her hand. "Violette, all's I'm saying is it seems like a… long shot. To me."

I give her a glare. "Well, if you can think of something else outside of calling Uncle Gray, tell us."

Jessie slumps down on her bed and rests her chin in her hand. *I feel the same way, Jess.*

The three of us are real quiet, lost in our own, similar thoughts, I'm pretty sure. Victory must have picked up our mood, because she plops down in the middle of us and gives a big sigh. For all the world, sitting here makes me think of being at a wake over at McCarty's Funeral Parlor in Blaylock.

My phone rings and breaks the silence like an icicle smashing against the window after an Ozark storm. "Hey, Junior. What're you calling so early for? Sun's barely walking around up there."

"My daddy took an early morning run to the feed store. Just got back. He told me all the talk's about your house being attacked by bear hunters last night. Really? Stupidest thing I ever heard of."

"Town's already talking about that?" I ask.

"You know what this place is like, Vi. Dumb-as-a-stump deputy's been blabbing all over Price's Tavern this morning, probably on his way home from work. Sheriff's got no rules; you know, protocol; so everybody's heard about y'all's house being shot up."

I sigh. "Well, it's true enough. And what you said about it being stupid? Exactly what I said to that useless policeman. You won't believe it when I tell you. Listen up."

"THAT'S THE MOST FARFETCHED CROCK I ever heard from a cop, Vi," Junior says, after I tell him the whole story. "But bullet holes in your house are a game changer. I'm coming on over now. I want to examine that tree stand and those holes for myself."

"I appreciate it, Junie. See you soon."

I click off my phone and turn back to Mama and Jess.

"Junior's coming over. He's gonna have a look around that stand and the house."

"Uh, Violette?" Mama says.

"Yeah?"

"Y'all be mindful out there. I don't want anybody killed or anything, you hear? And that goes for... Victory too."

"I hear, Mama. We'll be careful."

She glances at her watch. "Well, just wanted to get that straight before I leave this morning. Maybe I shouldn't go, what with all this... danger."

"No, you go on. You're safer out with the ladies than here."

"Well, y'all stay in touch, hear?"

Jessie gives her a watery smile. "Sure thing. And I'll walk you to your car, Mama. Just pretend I'm Vi doing dangerous stuff."

I give my sister a look, but even so, she's warmed my heart a little.

About fifteen minutes later, the puppy pricks up her ears and runs to the front window. I hear Junior's breaks squeal, and she stares at me.

"You got somebody new to meet, Victory, and you're gonna love him too," I say, opening the front door. "Come on."

The puppy charges out the door, straight to Junior's truck, parked behind mine. I keep a close eye on the woods. "Hey, Junie. Real glad to see you."

When he reaches us, Victory does the wiggle-greeting. Her eyes go all far away when he gives her a mega ear-scratch. "Some pup. I'd sure like to have me one of these."

"I know."

Junior shifts what I know is a handgun in his pocket. "Let's take a look at that stand."

Him and me, we slog across the front yard over to Sinclair Woods. Victory wants to run ahead of us, but I hold onto her collar. "Stay, Victory," I tell her, and she pretty much minds, even after I let her go.

Junior keeps his eyes locked on the woods but says, "That pup's smart. She's gonna be your bodyguard, Vi. Mind my words."

"That's what Mr. Ferguson said, too."

I got a feeling Junie and I are talking to ease our minds from what could be pretty dangerous stuff in those woods. Funny how heads work, time to time.

When we reach the trees, a few drops of water plop on us from drenched leaves. I wipe the back of my neck, and Victory shakes her body couple of times. Junior, he just ignores it, but his eyes? They shift right and left the whole time, and he keeps his hand in his pocket.

"Here's the tree, Junie. Over here," I say, in words that come out a whisper.

He puts another hard stare around the soggy woods, then examines the tree stand. "You're right about this being brand-new, Vi."

"So what do you think?"

"It's what *you* think. I mean, leaving a big clue on this property, where you can get dead if you're not a Sinclair, is like... crazy stupid. So the question is, *why'd* they build it?"

"It's what I've been trying to figure out. Did they build this stand only to scare us? Or to get Uncle Gray riled up?"

"Like we've said before, they'd be outta their heads to mess with Gray Sinclair, Vi. Anybody who had a lick of sense wouldn't do that." He lets go a breath. "Well, there's sure no clues here now, what with the storm last night." He rubs his burr haircut. "Since the cops won't do a thing, you gotta get Gray involved."

"I know, and I agree with you about that—for once. But listen. Now Mama *doesn't* think we should call Uncle Gray. She says there'll be too much gossip... or whatever, when he agitates everybody."

He looks at me and says nothing for a few seconds. "What's with her? Things are totally different from when we—well, you— hatched our plan. Doesn't she get it? I mean, a tree stand aimed right at your house? Your shot-up house?"

I look at the leaden sky, then back at Junior. "Don't know. But I *do* know she's acting just like she did those weeks back when I wanted to report Dale to the sheriff. She's real scared of something, Junie, and we need to find out what it is. Could help us with what's going on."

"Yeah, or get somebody killed even sooner."

A soft breeze kicks up, and a shower of droplets falls on us from soaked pine needles. Junior and I brush them off our faces. I reach over to Victory and run my hand down her wet back. "Uh," I say, "you find out anything else from Jake about Dale and the fights?"

"I was gonna talk about it inside. Never know who could be hiding out here."

I put my hand to my mouth. "Oh. You're right. Finished?"

Junior holds up his phone. "Yup. Lots of photos."

"Good. Hope Jessie's still home. She needs to be part of this conversation, what with Rucker *and* Jewel in the soup pot now."

When we head to the house, Junior walks behind me, but I know he's keeping a watch back to the woods. Though Victory bounds ahead, she stops every few seconds for us to catch up. Our feet make sucking sounds as we slog through soaked grass. I turn around and look at Junie. He nods, but it's not me he's seeing. Hand still in his gun pocket, Junior's eyes never stop taking in the dripping countryside all around us. He's scaring me, but in a strange way I feel safe as I did when my daddy was alive.

Victory leaps up the front steps and waits for us on the porch. Even with so much worry, I'm warmed inside. This pup already knows she's home.

"Look here, Junie," I say, pointing to a spot right under the eaves. "See those three bullet holes? Other one went into our bedroom, like I told you on the phone."

"Jesus. You're in a whole lot of trouble, Vi."

"Don't I know it."

I open the front door and yell, "Hey, Jessie?" Where are you?"

"In our room. What'd Junior think of that stand?"

"He's here now. You have time to come on in the kitchen and have a chat?"

"Sure. Out in a sec."

I shut the door behind Victory and Junior, then throw the deadbolt. It feels safe and secure here in the house, but that could change in a heartbeat with another bullet slamming through a wall or window.

Junior glances around the front room, then cracks his knuckles. "Where's your maw?"

I nod my head toward outside. "Off to a ladies' something-or-other with Mrs. McCord. C'mon, let's go to the kitchen."

"Smells good in here," Junior says. "Like fresh coffee."

"Want a cup?" I ask, turning toward the coffee pot. "Looks like Jess just made some."

Junior sits down and brushes a couple of crumbs off the table. "Sure."

"I'll get it," my sister says, sashaying into the kitchen from the hall. She pours each of us a mugful. I watch steam swirl like the fog in Sinclair Woods.

"Hey, Junior," Jessie says. "How's it going? Haven't seen you guys on the field yet."

"We start next week. You cheerleaders sure get out there sooner that we do."

"Yeah, but most of us girls like to get together. You know, practice on our own."

Junior chuckles. "Coach David wouldn't know how to act if our football team told him what you just said." He shakes his head. "Goes to show the difference in guys and girls."

Jessie nods. "Yeah, well, you're right on that one."

Junie lifts his cup to Jess as a thank you, takes a sip, and sets it down. "Okay, here's the deal. Y'all know Jake's had some... contact with Rucker the f... uh, Hicks. Well, last night up Hog Back at Mountain Man Bar, old Rucker told Jake and some other guys the dog ring's *ready to roll*. That's code for what these slime-buckets call a dogfight. Awful stuff 'cause it's a test fight between two fifteen-month-old puppies; it's their first time in the ring, and the winner goes on to the next stage."

Jessie raises her eyebrows. "And if they don't make it to the next stage?"

Junior glances down at Victory on the floor next to him. "Well, that's why Vi found this pup in the condition she was in."

Jess grimaces. Got a notion she's as sorry as I am to hear the answer.

Junior clears his throat. "Anyway, this syndicate is from Kansas City—Missouri, not Kansas. They're fixing to restart the fights on a regular basis now that their money's in place and the dogs are ready. Jake said they put in somewhere near a million bucks."

"Yeah, but is Dale part of it?"

Junior looks real long at each of us, dragging it out.

My brain starts to buzz. "Come on, Junie; let's hear what you know."

"Well, old Dale's in about as deep as it gets. He runs their shadow kennel, thanks to Rucker, who got him the job."

Jessie pops a purple bubble. "What's that?"

"A front for the *illegal* kennel where the fighting dogs are kept in a secret location, of course. Shadow kennel's strictly out in public for everybody to see, and it's for the law to check over and say it's on the up-and-up. The dogs in there only do weight pulls, stuff like that; you know legal stuff." Junior puts his coffee mug on the table. "And I almost forgot something. These dogs are called *PR dogs*, like in public relations? It's for keeping the public happy while bad things are going on undercover."

Jess crosses her legs, making her chair creak. "Wow. Crazy stuff I never knew."

A shiver tracks up my spine at what Junie just told us. Jess is right; crazy as the devil doing the Texas two-step and twice as mean. "Okay. So now that we know about Dale and the fights, what do we do? Go to Uncle Gray or try to set him up on our own?"

Junior shakes his head real slow. "Damned if I know, Vi. I see it both ways, and either one could be a deathtrap."

I nod to my sister. "Jess?"

"Way I figure, the more folks involved, more dangerous it gets for us. And with Uncle Gray being like he is... guess I'm saying to go for it on our own; see what happens."

"I think I'm with Jess on this one, Junior. Also, we gotta be getting close to those fights starting up. What are you thinking?"

He shrugs. "It's pretty near pissin' in the wind, you ask me. But you're right on one thing, Jess. Bringing in Gray adds another layer. So... how about this for starters? We keep our phones fully charged." He glances at me, then says, "Something I'm bad about. And make sure *all* doors stay locked, vehicles included. We don't go anywhere sketchy alone. Hear that, Vi?"

I nod.

"And we report back *anything* suspicions, no matter how insignificant we think it is. Deal?"

"Deal," Jess and I say together.

Jessie's eyes get all big. "I keep thinking about Jewel. If she isn't careful, she's gonna find herself in a real bad place too. I need to help her."

Junior puffs out a mouthful of air. "My advice? Stay out of it. More you get involved, worse it could be for us, including you."

Jessie has that deer in the headlights look, but she keeps her mouth shut. I feel sorry for her and Jewel too.

"So," I ask, "when do we put a move on these guys, at least on Dale?"

"Needs to be soon. I got football practice starting, and that'll take most all my time. Daddy's already bellyaching about my work hours having to be cut back on account of it. Hell, I bet he's glad me and Amberleigh broke up. Now I got more time for helping around the farm."

My sister flips her hair from one side to the other. "My advice? Don't get involved with her again. She did you a favor by breaking up. If we had tracks, she'd be from the wrong side of 'em."

I throw a glance at Junior, whose coffee mug is raised halfway to his mouth. He has an ironic look on his face. "More and more like your sister, Jess; more and more." And he smiles at us both.

Junior. Nicest boy I ever met and the truest friend.

25

My alarm clock rings, but I'm already awake and thinking about what Junie told us about Dale and Rucker. And I've got a crazy plan kicking around in my head. Junior has to go with me, but he won't be happy. I punch *Junior* on speed dial. "Hey, Junie," I say, when he picks up. "You work at eleven again today?"

"Naw. At one. Why?"

"I've got another piece of our plan. And would you just listen to it before you answer?"

"Maybe. Depends."

I knew he'd say something like that. Here goes nothing. "We need to carry ourselves back to Price's today. I mean, no time like the present, like you always say."

"Why? Why would you want to walk into Price's when you know Dale's gonna be there? It's foolhardy's what it is, Vi."

"There's a perfectly good reason besides getting a Coke."

"Oh, yeah? Well, lay it on me, because I sure as shootin' can't think of any."

I wish he'd stop using that phrase. "Okay, it's like this. We need to judge Dale's state of mind. Since I got the full treatment from him that day I went with you to the lumberyard, we should stop by again. See if he's calmed down. And, anyway, you're the one who said we have to focus on him. So…does that make sense to you?"

"No."

"Why not?"

"Because, Vi, a lot's happened between then and now, that's why. Also, he's linked up with old Rucker, and there's strength in numbers, especially when one of them is a full-fledged criminal. And last thing, his threats are getting a lot more regular."

"Well, I've decided to go to Price's, Junie. On the way now. You joining me or what?"

"Damn it, Vi. Sometimes you're as silly as a regular girl."

He gets silence from me.

"No, what I meant was…"

"I know what you meant. Just hurt my feelings *and* don't go with me to Price's. That's okay. See you sometime." I click off my phone and head to town, feeling wounded inside. I *am* a regular girl, and I *am* normal. If Junie can't see that, then nobody can.

When I drive through Bucktown's main street about twenty minutes later, Junior's truck is in front of the tavern with him in it. I park behind him, do a quick search for Dale's red truck, and spot it four places up from Junior's. I lock my doors and head for his side of the truck.

He lowers the window. "Vi, you know I didn't intend to make you feel bad."

What he said about me being silly like a regular girl gives me the upper hand, and we both know it, so I don't say anything.

"Aw, c'mon, Vi. I'm here, ain't I? You know I think you're a regular girl; only thing is, you got a serious right punch for a mite of a thing. Remember Eddie Coyne?"

I start laughing. Can't help it. "Yeah. Punched him right out for calling you fat when we were in first grade."

Uh-huh. "I rest my case, Miz Sinclair."

"All right, Junior."

I know he's working me over, but keeping on with that *regular girl* crack is not worth our friendship.

"I don't get why Dale's here every morning," I say as we step up on the sidewalk. "He doesn't work nights, does he?"

"Naw, days. But most of these guys are his buds, and he keeps track of what's happening around here. Listen, Vi. Weigh your words before speaking them and don't act mad or scared. Okay?"

"Okay."

I take a deep breath and can smell beer out here. The tavern door, scarred up from years of boots helping anxious hands to open it, is shut tight. Junior pushes it and lets me walk in first. Dim lights make the neon beer signs over the bar bright, almost glary.

About a dozen heads swivel toward the door, but I hone in on one; bald and cruel-looking, with menacing eyes focused on me. "Well, look who it isn't and with Bucktown's star football player too. Ain't that a pretty sight—or maybe just a sight?"

I give Dale a mean-eyed stare. He's keeping his honkin' big butt on the barstool this time. Doesn't want to tangle with Junior in front of his cronies.

"Hey, McKenna, you gonna give us a winning season?" one of the men asks.

"You bet, Mr. McGraw, or go down trying, anyway."

"That's the spirit, son," Mr. Elliott calls from across the bar.

Junior looks at me. "What can I get you, Vi?"

"A Coke's fine, thanks."

Junior saunters to the bar and squeezes in next to Dale while he orders. "How you been?" Dale asks.

"Just great. You?"

Dale takes a long drag on his cigarette then blows the smoke straight ahead, like he's trying to keep it out of Junior's eyes. "Nothing to complain about. Who're you going out with these days, McKenna, after that sweet thing, Amberleigh? I mean, I know who you're *not* going out with, if you catch my drift."

Junior shifts way too close in Dale's personal space. "No, I guess I don't catch what drift you're talking about?"

"Naw. It's your business, I reckon."

Junie's eyes bore into Dale's. "You reckon right."

"That'll be two Cokes, please," Junior says to the bartender, nice as my grandma's peach pie.

The man nods, reaches into the cooler then opens the drinks. "You got 'em, son."

"Thank you kindly," Junior says. He carries the Coke bottles to our table and grins at me. I raise my eyebrows, grin back, and don't care if Dale notices.

"So, you was givin' us the dogfight lowdown before them two walked in, Dale," one of the geezers at the bar says, nodding his head toward us. "Go on and finish up."

Dale takes a quick glimpse our way and pushes his shabby Kansas City Royals cap back. He picks up his bottle of beer, then sets it down without taking a swig. "Damned if I *really* know, Averill. Could be a crapload of hot wind, you ask me."

"No way. You already said there's too much talk out there for it being hot wind. Why, I hear tell the old FBI's sticking its nose in."

Dale takes a long swig of beer, then puts a look on Averill that could pierce the devil's heart. "Hell, there's been no FBI around here since forever. They won't darken this county's door. Y'all know that."

Junior and I look at each other. This whole time we've tried to figure out who in the law would listen to us and never once gave the feds any mind, mainly because they *don't* come around this county anymore, with 'shining mostly over and done with.

Junior chugs his Coke in about two swallows. "Well, Violette, how about another one?"

"Thanks, but I'm for hitting the road." I slide my chair back and stand up.

"Hey, you two," Dale growls. "I hear you been poking around Hog Back and such. Y'all better be real careful. Seems like danger's lurkin' 'round every corner in them parts."

Junior puts a puzzled expression on his face. "Huh, that's strange, Dale. I got real close kin up there, and they never talk about any danger, lurking or otherwise. Go figure."

A guffaw sounds from somewhere along the bar. "Looks like you got caught by the short and curlys on that one, Dale." In a singsong voice, the man says, "My mama always said to think before you speak."

"Shut your gob, Pinkus, or you're gonna have none *to* shut."

Junior stands up. "See y'all now, hear?"

I look back at the bartender. "Thank you." Really nothing to thank him for since Junior did already, but I need to get the last word in this place today.

Junior opens the door, and we step into overwhelming sunlight. "Okay, it was worth the trip, Vi. You were right. Now, how do we get in touch with the FBI?"

"Not sure. We gotta figure out the best way to contact them. You know, so they'll think we're serious and all."

Junie rubs his eyes hard. "We need somebody to do that for us. Somebody so serious the old FBI. would never think about saying no to them."

"Doc!" we say at the same time.

"Think she'll do it?" Junie says, taking the question right out of my mouth.

"Of course," I say, feeling about as sure as I would asking Uncle Gray for a favor. "Let me think on it; best way of talking to her and all."

"Good. That's good, Vi."

Not so sure, though. Hard to ask your boss for this kind of help. Especially when she's done so much already. Why is life so complicated?

"Hey, girls," Mama calls from the front room early this morning. "I'm leaving for my retreat. Won't be back till pretty late. Cold chicken's in the fridge, Vi. There's some late lettuce left in the garden and lots of tomatoes for a salad. Uh, y'all be careful now, hear? And that goes for seeing Victory's okay too. And, uh, nobody needs to walk me to the car this morning. I feel pretty safe."

I give a little wave. "Sure, Mama. Have fun."

Jessie turns to me. "Do you have fun at a retreat?"

"Don't know, but she seems awful happy to be going."

Jessie grabs her pink plastic purse and checks her money in a matching wallet. "I'm off with Seth and his daddy. We're driving to their cabin up Cooter's Mountain to go fishing. Only thing different in our plan is we're spending the night. I told Mama about it yesterday when you and Junior was... were at Price's." She gives me a look. "*And* Seth's bunking in with Pastor Akins's." She grins. "Thought you'd want to know."

"I *am* happy to hear that. Be sure and tell them hey from me, and have fun."

"I will. See you tomorrow afternoon," she says, snagging her backpack from the front room floor. She turns toward the door, pivots, and gives me a bear hug. "Stay safe around here, Vi. Please?" Before I can answer, she dashes out the door right as Pastor Akins' car drives up.

The house has gone quiet as Mama's church on a Monday afternoon, that is until Victory charges out of the kitchen, still licking her mouth from breakfast. "Hey, you fine puppy. We're going down to the cellar. With everyone gone, we got us a perfect time to search for those letters."

The pup pads back into the kitchen behind me. I unlock the cellar door and turn on the light. Hair raises on the back of my neck, causing me to shiver. Last time I walked down these steps, my mind was working overtime, what with the wails drifting up from the dark.

I reach the bottom and look around. Victory stands behind me, her muzzle in my hand.

The little cellar is windowless, damp, and cool. "Look at these shelves, pup," I whisper, because the room calls for whispering. Mama may not be an organized kitchen person, but she's a neat freak about this place. Each jar is sized from back to front and sorted with each label lined up for easy reading.

Shoving her stool along with my leg, I move from left to right, checking every inch of these friggin' shelves. After about fifteen minutes, I give it up. "This was a stupid waste of time, Victory. Mama's too clever to leave those letters, if that's what they are, lying around for God'n all to see."

I plop down on the stool, and the pup scoots over by me, laying her head on my feet. "How about we go upstairs? Nothing down here for us to find." When I stand, she leaps up fast, shoving the stool into my legs. *Thud!* I connect hard with the concrete floor, then hear something metallic roll under the shelf. Damn! If my butt could see stars, it would.

Long as I'm on the floor, I ought to find out what dropped. I flip over on my stomach and work my arm far as it can go under the shelf until something cold and smooth touches my hand. What the heck *is* this? I roll the object between two fingers. The bullet. I forgot to take it out of my shorts, the one Mama dug out of the wall the other morning. I tuck it deep in my pocket, then snap the pocket shut. Won't make that mistake again. I sigh and figure I'm about as dirty as I can get. Might as well search underneath the row of shelves long as I'm looking for letters.

I fish my phone from the other pocket and hit the light. About a million dust bunnies are under here, but something's gleaming white in that corner. *What's… oof… this? Maybe if I stretch my arm.* I reach something flat, and papery, and cobwebby. When I whip it out with my hand, the paper swishes across the floor, and hits the far wall. Cold sinks through me. *Be careful what you wish for:* Grandma's old-timey saying comes to my mind. I'd be happier if it hadn't.

Crawling across the gritty floor, I sit on the stool, then try to free my fingers and the envelope of cobwebs. This has been here a long time, or it got stuck in cobwebs when it landed against the wall.

The thin envelope is addressed to Mama, and the return address says, "H. Woodbine, P.O. Box 463, Branson, MO." Dale's mama was Hazel, and I know they have a mailbox, because Jess and I saw it up Hog Back. So why the post office box and why in Branson?

Like in a dream, I untuck the flimsy flap, ease the letter out, and a hint of lilac sweetens the air. I unfold the fragile paper and lay it upside-down on my lap. *Don't read this until you're sure you want to.* If I read the words written here, a whole world of hurt could happen. And then maybe Mama and Jessie and I will never find our way back to this very second before I witnessed the past and understood. But I turn it over and, though warning bells clang through my brain, I start to read:

June 3

My Dearest One,

I miss holding you in my arms and loving you, too. Please don't ever think I don't, because you're married now. At least you got a husband who is right kind and does not demand so much from you.

Like I said to you, my boys comfort me good, even if they were got by a man I hate. A man who hates me now. Walter's rough and mean, and what he wants from me he takes, and I got five boys because of it.

But my Cora, it's so different with us. I feel tender laying with you and I reckon you do with me, too. Don't you fret over being a bride. Just think about me when you have to be with John.

Anyway, enough of that talk. Law, it depresses me. I'm happy my forget-me-nots are doing fine by your porch. I see them blooming when I drive by, and they make me smile.

Can we find a meet-up place soon? Lord, I'm near crazy not being with you. I surely wait for the time that can happen.

Please let's still think on leaving this hell of a place. I hear tell that in Chicago nobody cares who or what you are. We can go and make a new life just like we talked about.

With my whole heart I love you,
Your own,
Hazel

The letter floats to the floor. I put my hand to my mouth and dry heave. Mama and *Mrs.* Woodbine. Lies. Both of their lives were—are—a pack of lies. Nothing's real. Everything's fake: a dishonest mother, a cheated-on father, and two daughters who're smack in the middle of a mess not of their making but still get a heap of misery every day because of it.

Mama was just a bride when she got that letter. She hadn't been married a month, and she was yearning over… Hazel. They had to be… lovers way before then. And Mrs. Woodbine, she was married too; her kids are lots older than us. If they'd gone on to Chicago, then Jess and me, we wouldn't be here.

White-hot hatred at Mama rises in my throat, and I gag again. She deceived Daddy; betrayed him and Jess and me too. My heart beats faster than that metronome sitting on the old piano at school. I glance around the room but see nothing. *What would I do if I had to marry a man because the times, they called for it?* That question goes fast as it comes. I won't let it linger, not now, maybe never.

I wipe away tears but can't make them stop falling. *Don't think about it anymore, Vi. Move on from this minute.* But somewhere far inside me, an uneasy thought stirs. *I'm gay like Mama. Mama's gay like me.* I drive it down deep, so deep it has to be gone, but when I look at myself inside and out, Mama will still be there.

Victory whimpers and licks my leg. "I know you been watching over me. Watching while I sobbed on this very bench where Mama sat and sobbed too. C'mon, girl. Time to do your business." I stand up on shaky legs and climb the cellar steps. This must be what ninety years old feels like.

I TREAD TO THE FRONT door quieter than quiet, and Victory pads after me, her nails *tick-ticking* on the old wood floor. When a harsh scraping sound comes from the porch, she lowers her head, raises her hackles, and growls. *Oh, Sweet Jesus! Dale knows about our mamas. That's why he's fixing to murder mine. I gotta get Daddy's old shotgun!* I sidle over to the cupboard, reach in, and snag it.

Standing sideways, I peek out the front window, lift the shotgun, and take aim at whoever's there. Who's there is Uncle Gray, starting to work on the rotten porch step. Couldn't have shot him anyway. My hands are shaking hard. I open the door too fast and nearly hit Victory. "Uncle Gray, I didn't expect you."

"Well, I told your mama I'd be here directly to mend this board, but it took me longer than I reckoned."

"No matter. It's good to see you."

He squints at me. "That so? Nobody's never much happy to see me, girl."

I lean against the door while he starts prizing up the bad board. "Hey, you hearing about any dogfights up Hog Back?"

"You're not fixing to stick your nose in that dangerous mess, are you, Violette?"

Huh-uh. "No. Just some talk at work's all. Doc's worried about it."

"If your vet knows what's good for her, she won't get near it, neither. Meddling with that syndicate makes cooking meth look like fixing food for a church picnic."

"Who do you think these people are? In the syndicate, I mean."

Uncle Gray puts a snaky look on me. "Violette, your mama's sometimes right about you in the trouble department. You always want to know too much about the wrong things." But he sighs, and I know he's going to give me something useful to gnaw on.

"I hear tell the gang that's fixing to run these fights are so cocksure of themselves 'cause they got a foolproof place to do it; no one seems to know where it is. And if a body gives them *any* trouble, their kind of... calling card, I guess, is shooting up their house or killing the barn animals first. You know, before they get real nasty."

My knees go all wobbly when Uncle Gray mentions shooting up a house. "But who's *doing* it?"

"Child, why do you want to know all this crap? Won't do anything but maybe get you into hurt the likes of which you never known. Recollect what I put to you up Sinclair Mountain a short time back? You gotta let well enough alone. Don't be rattling chains."

"I told you, Doc needs to know."

My uncle shakes his head like he's sure I've got nothing to shake in mine. "Word's out that criminal Hicks guy's heading up the local folks, and the no-good Woodbine bully's his right-hand man." He mashes a clod of dirt from his huge work boot into the old board and throws it off the porch. "You've already been Dale-beat pretty bad, so I'd leave it be if I was you, missy."

"But like I *told* you up Sinclair Mountain, if we can catch him in the act of running the fights, he'll go away for a devil's spell, and we'll be safe."

My uncle examines his gnarled hand. "Young'un, keep on the way you're headed, you're gonna wake up dead, like the saying goes around here. You *and* that Junior. Kid may be a linebacker and all, but I'd wager he don't know squat about the devilment in some folks in these hills."

"Then why don't *you* do something to help me, Uncle Gray, like I've asked before, being the head of us Sinclairs?"

Uncle Gray keeps his eyes down. "It's complicated, girl. I can't be seen… condoning the way you say you are. Though I haven't… nobody's actually seen you with a… female. So I reckon it's more like folks are guessing 'cause of that time in school." He puts a look on me that asks for more information. Sad to say, there's nothing to tell.

"I'm your niece. You're my uncle *and* clan head. You *owe* me protection, especially since we get none from the law in this county. Simple as that, Uncle Gray; simple as that. Doesn't matter if I'm gay or straight, black, white, or green. You took an oath to protect me as a *Sinclair*."

I hold my breath because, sure as a greased thunderstorm, I'm gonna get a head thump right quick. But it doesn't happen. Instead, he stares at me stern as can be, but not mean. Then he wipes his sweaty face with a tattered handkerchief and sits down on the top step.

"Young'un, you're gonna be the death of your mama with the kind of questions you ask and your... reckless decisions. It's no surprise you been a thorn in her side since you was the size of tadpole. I know this determined streak you have is because of your... affliction, like your aunt calls it. But child, it ain't a hero thing like you think; good chance your actions are gonna get you in an early grave, the way I keep saying."

I plop down on the step next to my uncle and stare at him with what I hope *is* determination.

He looks away fast, then focuses his eyes directly back on me, like he's deciding something. Rolling down the sleeves of his red checkered shirt, he buttons them even though it's getting hotter by the minute.

"Violette, your mama's... complicated. She was surprised when you came along and had no notion what to do with a baby. Why, Cora didn't think you'd happen at all."

"That was because she hardly ever had sex with my daddy, even though they were just married, wasn't it?"

"Damn, girl. Where you get such notions?"

"Why didn't Mama want to... sleep with Daddy? They had their own room but used twin beds. Mama always said Daddy snored. Only way she could sleep was to bury her head in a pillow. Weird thing is, I never once heard my daddy snore."

"What're you getting at, Violette?"

He answers my question with a question, and that's not lost on me. "What I need to know is why the Woodbines have a death wish for Mama and me. I never did him or Mrs. Woodbine any harm; didn't even know the woman. So, what's the deal with Dale?"

Uncle Gray pulls the handkerchief back out of his pocket and wipes his sweaty face. He turns it over, studies it like he's gonna find an answer, then returns it to the same pocket. "Law, girl, best not to go poking into other people's lives around here. Like I said, that can get you laid out on a marble slab over at McCarty's Funeral Parlor."

"I suppose it can, but the way I see it with Mama, Jess, and me? We're going to end up dead by Dale's hand if I don't do something to stop him. Who else is gonna do it?"

Uncle Gray, he puts his head in his hands, greasy hair hiding dirty fingernails. "Child, you don't have any notion what—"

"I have a letter."

He's suddenly all interest and ears. "From who?"

"From Dale's mama to mine."

"What kind of letter?"

I make Uncle Gray wait for his answer, then say real slow, "A love letter. They declare their love for each other and talk about how they plan on moving to Chicago. They were lovers, Uncle Gray. Lesbian lovers."

I swear his hand's shaking when he swipes at his nose. "I'll be. So it's come back to haunt us Sinclairs at last."

"Me, Uncle Gray. It's come back to haunt me, me and my little sister. There's information I need to keep all of us alive, and I know you recognize the truth of what I'm saying. Mama must have tried to save her lover's life what with the cancer eating her up and, of course, couldn't do it."

"That *is* about the truth of it, I reckon, Violette. God help us all."

"Why didn't you say something about all this years ago? Don't you see how it would have helped me, and Mama, too, maybe understand each other better? Aunt Zinnie said I needed to talk to Mama. But you're my blood, Uncle Gray. Why didn't you tell me what I needed to know after Daddy died and I grew up?"

My uncle puts a hard stare on me, and I know I've gone too far. Almost sure he's gonna box my ears, I lean as far away as I can from his hands. But they just hang there, almost like they're lost and don't know what to do.

"In those days, I was trying to protect my baby brother from your mama. He was broken, Violette, doubted his manhood. She told him how that Woodbine woman could do it better than him, and she was the only person who could fulfill her, stuff like that. I know for a fact he only stayed with your mama for you girls. He didn't want her to be the main influence on you."

His words jolt me like a cattle prod, but I gotta go on, get answers. "Where… where did they meet up, Uncle Gray? Mama and Hazel."

"Uh, sugar, I think I've gone a mite too far, like your Aunt Zinnie tells me sometimes."

He's never called me sugar the way my aunt does, and I know it's because he feels sorry for what he told me. Unexpected tears sting my eyes. "Please, Uncle Gray, this hurt has to stop for everybody. It's even spilling over on Jessie's best friend, Jewel, who's got a thing going on with Hicks."

He raises his eyebrows. "That little girl?"

Nodding, I say nothing.

He rubs the back of his neck and scrunches his eyes with arthritic fingers. "Well, it was all a bad scene." He pitches me a half-smile. "Isn't that what you youngsters say, *scene*? Or is that word old-fashioned these days?"

Uncle Gray's stalling for time. I get it and stay patient until he puts his thoughts together. "Mrs. Woodbine—Hazel—she came here as Walter's bride from Springfield, or some such place. More citified, anyway."

"Oh, I thought they were Ozark born and bred."

"The Woodbine clan was, but Hazel, she was a foreigner. Anyway, the two gals became friends, fast friends real quick, what with them being young women, even though Hazel was a mite older. Nobody thought a thing of it. Why would they? That is, until they started disappearing for long stretches of time and weren't to be found anywhere. Now their young'uns, y'all were tended to, what with kin and others to help out, but something wasn't right."

A memory charges through me, so strong it almost knocks me off the step. Mama gone for hours and Daddy home from work, worried sick that she had a mountain driving accident or something. And then, when she came home, there was a terrible fight about her leaving us alone, especially after dark, and where had she been, anyway? Mama wouldn't tell, and Daddy, he stormed out, banging the door behind him. Then it dissolves from my mind like smoke, a ghost raised from the past to bedevil me.

Uncle Gray unbuttons the sleeves of his shirt, rolls them up, then looks at me in a terrible way. I got a real bad feeling as to what's coming next. *I don't want to hear it.*

"The women, they were meeting... having sex in the Woodbines' root cellar. Nobody used it anymore; too far from the house." He lowers his head. "They had a bed in there and stuff on the walls to pretty it up and everything."

I gasp. The root cellar, the one Jess and I drove by is where they—I can't bring myself to even think that word—loved each other and made plans to leave here for Chicago. I gag, and my eyes water.

"You okay, girl?"

I hold my hand to my mouth and nod again. "But in the winter?"

"Root cellars stay pretty much same temperature year-round. Little colder then, but with heavy blankets and body heat…"

My uncle peeks at me and continues talking. "On one of his walks around the farm, Walter heard noises from behind that door and found them in bed, naked as the day they were born. Worse luck was the preacher happened to be with him. He threw them out of the church then and there. Blaylock Church is where they went in those days."

"Those days being when?"

Uncle Gray doesn't stop a second to think. "That was August, seven years ago. You remember those days? About the church mess and such?"

"Not much. I was only ten, and Daddy didn't make us go to church with Mama. But my daddy was shot on Thanksgiving Day, seven years ago. Right?"

"You might say that."

"I do say that, Uncle Gray, and I want to know why it was then and who killed him?"

"Now, child…"

A burst of fury explodes in me, in spite of fearing my uncle. "No! Don't you *child* me. I need answers now, Uncle Gray."

"You hear me good, Violette. *I* don't even know who pulled that trigger, and I was standing plumb next to your daddy. Nobody could see worth a damn; cloudy it was, and the woods were awash in mist."

"You know it was Dale, Uncle Gray. You know it!"

"Now, missy, there's no way to prove such a thing. My suspicions are he did it, with him being the orneriest man in these parts, but that'll not hold sway in a court of law, especially with Judge Sallee, who's got Sheriff Fletcher in his back pocket."

I won't stop. My mind's a blaze of heat, so white-hot I can scarce see. "He found out about our mamas being lovers, didn't he? He found out and put two bullets in my daddy, didn't he, Uncle Gray. Didn't he? Hazel, she begged her menfolk not to shoot Mama 'cause that would be the death of her, too, so they killed my daddy instead."

Uncle Gray stares straight ahead, not saying a word. He doesn't have to, because I've said them all. I've said every one there is to say. I look at the sky, and it's still there. My life's torn apart because of Mama being gay—gay like her daughter—and the sky's still there.

When I stop sobbing and hiccupping, Uncle Gray puts my hand in his rough and calloused one. We sit there on the sunny porch while the bees buzz, and the birds sing, and the world tends to its business all around us. The clock's turned back seven years for me and, I reckon, for my uncle too.

"So everyone knew… knows about Mama and her?"

Uncle Gray shakes his head. "No, not many. The preacher did, and he didn't talk. But your mama, she had some kind of breakdown after they got found out. It was a bad one. She wouldn't budge much out of your cellar for months. You recall any of that?"

"Yeah, I recall."

"Well, the years wore on like they do, and I figured the whole thing was long dead and forgot. Those Woodbines, they were up Hog Back, and far as I could tell, the women never met again until your mama went there to pray for Hazel on account of the cancer. Even if she could have done something to help, Hazel was too far gone and died not long afterwards."

Uncle Gray sighs and puts my hand back in my lap, so gentle. "When his mama died a few months back, that crazy Dale started acting up. I expect your mama promised she could cure Hazel, and he counted on that. But when your mama couldn't keep her promise, and Hazel passed on, Dale started putting the torment on you. That's when I thought, 'Here it comes back to haunt us.'"

"Me, Uncle Gray, back to haunt me."

"I know, sugar, and I'm sorry about the way I've treated and downright neglected you a time or two."

I let that one go.

"It won't happen again; it surely won't."

I believe him and am grateful for it.

Uncle Gray takes a breath, hesitates, then starts to speak. "Violette, after you was beat so bad, I went on up Hog Back. Told Dale I'd kill him with my bare hands, weight him down, and pitch him in Lake Taneycomo if he ever touched you again."

His words stun me to my core. "But you never—"

"No, I never told you on account of you being the way you are. Now I'm not meaning this gay stuff. No. It's you take too many... unjustified risks all the time. I thought telling you'd get your ire up; set you off into more danger just to show folks you could handle things on your own. 'Cause of your affliction and all."

"Uncle Gray—"

He puts his hand out. "I won't call it that anymore." He nods, real solemn. "Not dignified. Fact is, I ran into the sheriff right after I put the threat on Dale. Told him I was sick of way you was being treated. He said there's nothing he could do. You had no proof about Dale; his word against yours. Stuff like that."

"He told me the same thing."

"I know, child. You tried to tell me up Sinclair Mountain, and I wouldn't listen."

"Does… does Mama know all this?"

"I told her, Violette, like I'm telling you now. She has no notion what to do. Way it stands is, I'd have to kill Dale, and the sheriff, then probably other Woodbines that come after you, them being out for revenge. It'd be a major blood feud."

I nod slow at my uncle. That's the worst thing that can happen. I know it. Everybody knows it. I need to breathe, but breath won't come.

"Sugar, this is a tough old place, and a body grows up hard here. And because I knew that firsthand but didn't act on it with you young'uns, I've got some redemption to do with my family."

"Uncle Gray—"

"No, it's time to make things right. Damn if this craziness ain't gonna stop so another generation of womenfolk won't be tormented. I don't like this lesbian stuff, Vi. It killed my baby brother. But folks shouldn't be murdered for it like your daddy was, even if they're not Sinclairs."

Uncle Gray chuckles, but there's not a touch of joy in it. "Even with everything? You and me, we're so much alike. Maybe that's why we knock heads all the time. I… didn't want to admit it these past years, you being… the way you are and all. But I was wrong.

You're the best of us, Violette Ross Sinclair. The best of this clan, like your daddy was before you. Like I'll never be."

That's the most powerful thing Uncle Gray's ever told me, and my tears stir up again, and I don't want them to. But when I look into my uncle's worn-out eyes, his tears glisten right back at me. We grab each other and hold on tight, and I finally feel like a truly born and bred Sinclair.

28

Junior skims a pebble three hits across the Bucktown pond, a good place to meet up if you want to talk in private. "Now that you told me about your maw and Mrs. Woodbine, you haven't said squat about how *you're* doing this morning."

"I'm okay, Junie. The terrible shock's over." But I'm really not and maybe never will be. I scratch at a bite on my leg just short of making it bleed.

Junior stretches out on his back, and I wonder how he can do that, what with ticks all over creation. "Better to know the truth is what I think. If you want my opinion," he says.

"Yeah, I guess. It's gonna take time. Gotta tell Jess when she gets home from fishing today; hope she'll take it all right."

"Aw, Jess? She's tough. Tough as they come. She'll be okay. Uh, listen, Vi, the syndicate's first dogfight's this Thursday night. Jake told me right before I left to meet you. He got it from Rucker, so it's probably true."

A zap of panic shoots through me. "What are we gonna do with only two days to get our plan... solid?"

He sits back up and glides another pebble across the water. "Here's what I think, Vi, but tell me if you don't agree. We talk to Doc like we planned; ask if *she'll* get in touch with the FBI. I don't think she'd mind, her having lots of… authority. What do you think?"

"Yeah, we're kind of late, but Doc'll be okay with it, I think. I'll see her first thing at work this afternoon and ask her."

WHY DID I TELL JUNIE I'd ask Doc about helping? My hands are sweating, and I'm shaky inside. All the way to the clinic, I practice what to say to Doc about the FBI. Now that the time's come, I'm worried about getting her involved. I open the door and try to ignore the butterflies in my stomach. "Hey, Loretta."

"Hey, yourself, Vi. Hope you're doing good this beautiful day."

"Yes, I am, thanks," I lie. "You know where I can find Doc?"

"I think she's in the Trauma Room. Lloyd Wiggins brought in a hit-and-run dog little while ago; she's tending to it now."

"Thanks, Loretta," I say and head for the Trauma Room, thinking of Victory in there not long ago.

"Hey, Doc," I say in a quiet voice. "Is it going to be okay?"

"Oh, hi, Vi," she says, drying her hands with a paper towel. "Thankfully, yes. The car nudged him enough to cause some pretty bad contusions and abrasions, but nothing life-threatening. The other good news for a hit-and-run is that Lloyd's going to adopt him, his old lab Molly having just died."

"Aw, that's great, Doc. Uh, do you have a minute to chat?"

"Certainly I do. My one o'clock isn't here yet." She smiles and puts her hand on my shoulder. "How can I help you?"

"That's quite a story," she says, after listening to my tale of Rucker, and Mama, and Mrs. Woodbine, and all the reasons why Dale hates me. "It's like a book or a film."

"Yeah, except it's my real life. Only nobody'd believe it."

"Well, I do. Remember my telling you there was something in the back of my mind about your... situation all those years ago?"

I hold my breath for a second. "Yeah, Doc."

"It came to mind while you were talking just now. I was asked to be an expert witness in a deposition, you know, a meeting with the two side's lawyers to see if someone has to stand trial."

I nod like I know what she's talking about, but really I've never heard of it.

"Well," Doc says, "this depo involved Dale and cruelty to dogs. When I finished testifying, your mother spoke on Dale's behalf, as a character witness."

I must have a stunned look on my face, because Doc stops her story and says, "From what you've just told me about Hazel and your mother's... relationship, I imagine Dale's mom asked yours to speak for him."

"Yeah, I reckon that's what happened," I mutter.

"But here's the interesting part, Vi. After your mom gave a glowing speech on what a fine young man he was, the court lawyer was very harsh with *her*. I don't recall exactly what he said, but the gist of it was that she had some terrible things in her own past, making her a weak witness for Dale. I felt sorry for your mom. After all, she wasn't the one in trouble, and that lawyer was filthy to her."

I feel sorry for Mama too. "Yeah, guess that's Hitchens County justice at work, then and now. So what happened to Dale?"

She blows out a large breath. "Exactly what you'd expect. He got off with only a warning to stay away from any dogs, which he promised to do. It was a joke, a waste of my time, and no change in his treatment of animals. So, yes, I'll be happy to contact the FBI and will let you know soon as I hear. These thugs need to be stopped, and I'm here to help you make that happen."

"Thanks." Nothing to add.

"Uh, Vi? I want... to be honest with you." She rubs the covered motorcycle on her left wrist. "There's another reason I need to help. In my wild days—I told you a little about them—I dated a guy who thought he was above the law. You know the kind."

I nod. "Lots of them around here, Doc."

"One afternoon, I was riding on the back of his motorcycle. He was going too fast as usual. A small black dog was in the middle of the country road. I... I screamed for him to brake, but he paid no attention. He hit the dog; killed it outright. When we stopped a few minutes later, I was sick everywhere. When I asked him why he hit the dog, he told me if the dog was too stupid to move, then it deserved what it got."

My hand is over my mouth, and I don't know when I put it there.

"I got off that cycle, didn't say another word, and walked home. It was at that moment my life changed. Everything became clear, and with support from a couple of people, as I mentioned earlier, I never looked back at those days, except to evaluate how and why my new life was proceeding."

"And you've been helping animals since that happened."

"Something like that."

I shake my head, too stunned to say anything. Doc, she never says a word about her personal life, and then she tells me this. "That… that's a terrible thing to happen to someone, anyone," I mutter. "No wonder you're so dedicated. Not that you wouldn't be anyway," I say too fast.

She glances down, probably at her wrist, I'm guessing, seeing through the white material to the motorcycle that pretty much determined her fate. And the fate of thousands of animals, if you look at it like that.

"So, Vi," she says softly but with a hard edge, "bring on the FBI, and let's get these bastards in prison."

All my butterflies have suddenly disappeared.

THE WHOLE WAY HOME FROM work, I'm all wound up. Doc told that story *for* me, too; for my new life that's beginning right now. I have to think on what she said real hard. All through supper, I can hardly eat.

Jess watches me like a hawk ready to swoop. "What's up with you, Vi? How come you're not eating? Roast beef; your favorite."

I peek over at Mama, then give my sister an ugly glare. "Just an upset stomach, Jess. Don't you ever have them?"

She gets a real hurt look on her face. "Yeah, sometimes."

"Sorry."

"It's okay," she says in a small voice.

"No, it isn't, sis. That was mean."

"I like how you girls are so nice to each other these days," Mama says. "Your daddy, he'd be real proud."

"Yeah," Jess and I say together, then smile at each other.

After we finish the dishes, and Mama's gone to the front room, I say to Jess, "I need to show you something. It's gonna be hard, but promise you'll listen and not get too upset. Okay?"

"I'll try. What is it, Vi? You're not leaving home yet, are you?"

"No, nothing like that. Let's go into our room." I shut the door. My body feels tight as a coil when I open my chifforobe drawer and put my hand on the letter. "You need to read this. It'll explain some of Mama's... behavior and an awful lot about our lives too."

My sister's eyes move quick over the words, like she has to get it over with. Puts me in mind of taking bad-tasting medicine. "Is this a joke? Tell me it isn't the truth, Vi."

"It's the truth. We needed to know the truth, Jess."

"How did you...?"

"I was in the cellar, looking for letters. You were gone up to Seth's fishing cabin, and Mama was..." *Get to it, Vi. You got Jessie hanging on here.* "Anyway, I dropped that bullet out of my pocket, and it rolled under the shelf. Found the letter when I reached under to get it."

"Mama and Mrs. Woodbine? This whole time we thought it was Mama and *Mr.* Woodbine. Now I wish it was."

"I know what you mean, Jess."

The letter flutters to the floor. When I look at Jessie's face, pain is carved into it, and she seems older than her years.

"Jess," I say, then stop and shake my head. I need to start over. "Uncle Gray stopped by here yesterday; you know, to fix the rotten board?"

She gapes at me, but I don't think what I'm saying is registering.

"Well, he… he told me some stuff about Mama and Mrs. Woodbine; hard stuff, but you need to know it. Okay if I tell you?" I ask her gentle, but still don't think she's paying me any mind. "Jess?"

She gazes out our bedroom window, over to old Mr. Willis's field. Same field where Dale shot him dead. "I hear you, Vi. Wish to sweet Jesus I couldn't, but I hear you."

"Okay. I'm fixing to tell you easy as I can."

Jess, she listens to me. I can tell it from her eyes, and it pains me to recount what Uncle Gray told me. When I get to the part about their lovers' hideout, Jessie covers her mouth. "In that old root cellar we drove by? Disgusting."

Jewel and Rucker doing it in his tent float through my mind, but I let it go. "What were they supposed to do?" I ask. "They loved each other and wanted to be together."

"Yeah, but—" Jessie glances at me, stops, and gets busy scratching a mosquito bite on her leg.

Heat rises to my face. I can't believe I'm defending Mama after the terrible heartache she's caused. But what she had to go through—all those years of loving, and hurting, and yearning for someone she'd never be with again—must have been hell itself. That old Miss Havisham flashes into my mind once more. Mr. Dickens most surely could have been writing about Mama and Mrs. Woodbine.

"Well, Jessie," I say, bending over to retrieve the letter. "What's done is done. No taking any of it back. You and me? We're left to deal with the damage caused by Dale. Damage because our mamas loved each other in a time and place where it couldn't happen without consequences."

My sister presses her eyes hard with purple-nailed fingers. "Yeah," she says, so soft. "Consequences we have to deal with, or we're all gonna die."

I scoot over next to Jessie on her bed and wrap my arm around her thin shoulders. "I'm not fixing to let that happen to us; to you, or Mama, or me. We don't deserve it, and between Uncle Gray, and Junie and me, old Dale? He doesn't stand a chance."

Now if I only believed that myself, things might be looking up.

MAMA TOPS UP HER COFFEE mug, then peers at me with puffy, red-rimmed eyes. "What'd you girls talk about late into the night? I heard you yammering on in there until I fell asleep."

I shrug. "Aw, just gal-talk, Mama. Did you know Jewel's going with that Rucker Hicks?"

"I heard a thing or two about it in town a few days ago." She shakes her head slow. "That girl's not thinking with her brain, if you catch my drift."

"Yeah. I surely catch it and am worried for her too."

She looks at me, starts to say something and hesitates a second. "You know that Hicks guy is kin to Dale."

"What? He's what? What kind of kin?"

"Not quite sure, Violette. It's been a long spell. Well, what I mean is, he's like a second cousin on his... mama's side, something like that."

"But I thought Mrs. Woodbine was a foreigner—Springfield or some such place." *Oh, God. What have I done? Think of an answer to what she's gonna say.*

"Now, how would you know that, Violette?"

"Mama, stuff like this, you hear it around. You know."

"No, Violette, I don't know that." She puts a squint on me that ices up my blood. "Who you been talking to, anyway?"

"I... nobody, I been talking to nobody."

"You been palavering with Gray when he mended that porch board, ain't you?"

"Why are you asking me these questions? You got something to hide?"

Mama offers up another frosty glare, sets down her mug, and heads outside. Her work shoes flop on each step and put me in mind of her garden in winter, wilted and withered away.

My phone rings a few minutes later, and I see it's Doc. *Did I make a mistake and it's not really my day off?* "Hey, Doc."

"I have some news, Vi."

My heart does a big flip.

"I've been in touch with the Springfield branch of FBI, and they were *very* helpful. Evidently, they've had a presence around this area, anticipating the syndicate's start-up. The thing is, though, they couldn't find the location for the fights. The gentleman I talked to said a lot of the locals either don't know or are keeping that information close to their vests."

"I'm not surprised about that, Doc."

"Neither am I, and actually, I'm amazed you found it, what with all the nooks and crannies in these mountains."

"Me too."

"So here's what's happening. A Mr. Connelly will call you to get directions. Is that okay?"

"Sure."

"I thought so. Then they'll take a run up Hog Back Mountain, determine that's the site, and make preparations for tomorrow night. Talk about cutting it close to the bone."

"Yeah. I'll call Junior right away. Thanks, Doc."

"You're more than welcome. Only one thing? Promise to be *very* careful from here on out."

"Promise; I truly do. See you soon."

I hope like everything that's true.

Before I can speed-dial Junie, my phone rings again. Coffee sloshes out of the cup onto my clean shorts. Blocked number. Must be Mr. Connelly. I hurry out to the porch and plop down on the top step, feet on Uncle Gray's mended board. "Hello?... Yes, sir, I was expecting your call... Yes, sir... No, sir, I understand... Do I need to meet you...? Oh... We'll be sure to follow what you're saying... Thank you, Mr. Connelly... I surely hope so too... Bye now."

"So that's it, Junior," I say, about a minute after talking to the agent. "One thing he said a couple times was how we *cannot* be up there tomorrow night. It could complicate things and put us in danger, and they've got enough of that to deal with. Also, we need to be in a public place where we can be seen during the raid. They're smart, Junie, real smart. How about we meet up at Price's at eight-thirty? That way, folks can see both our trucks when they're driving by; ditto for us in the tavern."

"Suits me, Vi. See you there, and let's hope it goes our way. It'd sure as hell be good to get this bother behind us once and for all."

"Amen to that, like my mama says."

"Seems even the air's waiting for tonight to come," my sister says, dangling her legs off the front porch. "All hot, and still, and holding its breath for the terrible storm to get here."

"I surely know what you mean, Jess."

"Uh, you think me and Jewel can go with y'all to Price's later? It could help her, being there and all."

"Well, I don't care, and Junior won't, and neither will Price's. Heck, they let three-year-olds in long as they don't get around the bar. Actually, now I think about it, that's a smart idea where Jewel's concerned, so tell her it's fine by us."

Jess won't look in my eyes. "I already did, soon as you told me about being out in public tonight."

My heart revs up. "Jess, please tell me you didn't say—"

She throws both hands, palms up, in the air. "No! Listen. We made plans to go to the Shine like we do sometimes, but it'd be better if we could all be together. And Vi, I didn't tell her *anything* about what's happening tonight. You gotta believe me. It's just that she's been my best friend since forever, and all's I wanted to do was help her, but I'd never say a thing that might put you or Junior in that kind of trouble. She still thinks we're going to the Shine."

Jessie, she's talking fast, and her face is red, and sweat glistens across her forehead. God, I hope she's not lying. "Okay, okay," I say, backing down and wanting to trust her more than anything right now, "but I think it'd be better if you guys go on in Jewel's car; seems more natural that way. We're meeting up at Price's at eight-thirty."

She pushes damp hair off her forehead and nods. "So, I'll have Jewel pick me up by eight o'clock. And please believe me. About me not telling her anything. I...wouldn't do that to you guys."

"I believe you, Jess."

I hope to high heaven she's not lying.

MY HANDS ARE SWEATING, AND I can't get enough air on the drive to Price's this evening. I keep telling myself it'll be okay, that this is the only way to be done with Dale. Trouble is, I scarce believe a word of it.

I drive slow down Main Street. Otis, the only mechanic in town, is sprawled under a dilapidated car parked at the curb, and the Hollerer brother and sister are on the corner talking loud enough to wake the dead at some poor guy. I don't know what their real names are. They're the Hollerers to everybody in Bucktown, 'cause holler all the time is what they do. I shake my head and wonder how the whole world can look the same when you know your life might change forever real soon. And everything goes on just like it was.

Price's Tavern is coming up on my right, and there are two spaces in front. A couple of people mill around the front door, but nobody I know. My stomach gives me a zing, and I slow way down and glance in my rearview mirror. Junie's right behind me. Talk about timing.

We take the parking spaces, and both of us check our doors to be sure they're locked.

Junior's wearing a pair of khaki shorts and a dark blue T-shirt with a bullseye on the front. Suppose he doesn't see the humor in his choice of shirt. "You ready for whatever happens tonight, Vi?"

"Not hardly. I'm scared to death. Uh, thanks for letting the girls tag along with us."

Junior nods his head toward an ancient car belching fumes and bumping along the street. "Here they come now. I just hope they behave themselves."

"Well, look at it this way. The agent wanted people to notice us. With those two around, no worries about that."

He chuckles in his quiet way.

Jess hits us with a big smile a couple of minutes later. "Hey, talk about timing. Here we all are!"

She's way too happy for the situation; guess that's how you act a week or so shy of sixteen.

"Let me get the door for y'all girls," Junior says, strolling up to the tavern.

"Wait." Jewel holds out her arm to stop him. "I... uh... want to say something to you both before we go in. I been worrying over this, what I'm gonna say, I mean, and I need to say it." She takes a deep breath. "What I said about the two of you up Hog Back; you know what I mean?"

I try to keep my face neutral. "Yes."

"Well, it was bad of me; real bad, and I should of apologized soon as those words came out of my mouth, but I didn't. I am now, apologizing, and hope y'all accept it."

Junior gives me a look. "We do, Jewel; don't we, Vi?"

I nod and sort of smile.

He gives her shoulder a quick squeeze. "You were brave to say something, so we'll forget about it now."

"Thanks," she says in almost a whisper.

I lower my head a touch. He's nicer than I am.

When we walk in, smoke's so thick that the whole tavern's blue and so is Patsy Cline, wailing her heart out on the jukebox about falling to pieces. I can't help but think back on the morning Dale made me feel like a worthless piece of crap in here. Only a few weeks ago, but it could be a lifetime with all that's happened since.

"C'mon, Vi," Jessie says, "you and me are going to the table together." She takes my arm and makes a show of being with her sister, and damn Dale to hell, I never felt better in these Ozarks than I do at this moment.

Jewel points to a table. "Is that one too close to the bar for me and Jess, Junior?"

"Naw, they don't care where y'all sit, probably not even at the bar long you got money to pay. Is it Cokes all around?"

"Yes," the girls say together.

"Okay, and I'll snag some chips from the bar too. Be right back, ladies."

The girls rotate where they're sitting a couple of times before settling at the table. I smile inside, thinking how much fun it is to be with young teenagers again. All the trouble in my life made me forget; that's not gonna happen anymore.

"This joint's jumpin' tonight," I tell Junior when he returns. "At least you can see who's not up Hog Back. We got almost the last table, and people are jammed around the pool table something crazy. Is it always like this on a weeknight?"

He stuffs wadded up money in his shorts pocket. "Not that I remember. I'm thinking word's out about the fights, and folks are waiting to hear about them down here."

"And I'm thinking you're right."

The girls are munching their chips and giggling like crazy when Junior nods his head toward the door. "Take a look at who's walking in, Vi. Those guys are so FBI they could be from a movie."

Lean and sharp-eyed, the two men are dressed in khaki pants and short-sleeved shirts that have been starched and ironed so no wrinkle would dare show up. They have a quick manner; nothing but business. I whisper to Junior. "Talk about putting the stare on all us locals."

He raises his eyebrows but says nothing. Just watches them close.

An antique couple at the table next to us stands up slow as a July snowstorm. The lady thumps her walker around tables, and her husband follows, helped by a cane. "Evenin', gentlemen," the old man says in a voice that sounds like wispy smoke looks. He tips an imaginary hat. "Table right over yonder with your names on it."

One of the men glances toward us. "Kind of you, sir. Take care now, hear?"

Jessie shivers. "They're gonna sit too close to us. They'll see how young we are."

"It's okay," Junior says, real soft. They haven't come for you; won't even notice y'all."

The men step to the table and pull out chairs that make a heavy scraping noise in the suddenly silent tavern. Lurleen, the gum-chomping, overworked waitress, scurries over.

"What can I do you for?" she asks, in her heavy Ozark accent.

"Couple of burgers and Cokes," the older-looking guy says.

Nodding, she tucks her pencil behind an ear, raises her head high, and marches to the bar. If it wasn't so hushed in here, I'd have a chuckle watching her taking this order so serious.

Lurleen never takes her eyes off the men while she snags two Cokes from the little fridge under the bar. "Here you go, gents," she says, delivering them with half a smile. "Hope they taste same as where y'all come from."

The younger man tips the bottle toward her and doesn't speak a word. He doesn't smile, either.

"I swan," I mutter to our table. "This is like watching a movie."

The tavern door flies open, and two mountain men slam in. "There's been a raid," the first one inside yells. "Raid on the fights up Hog Back."

The other man, dressed in a wife-beater and too-large coveralls, joins in. "Yup. Declan's talking gospel. We heard tell they carted off about twenty dogs, too, but some got away with their owners." When the men focus their eyes long enough to spot the feds, they stop dead.

I push my icy Coke away; I don't have a need for it now, because my insides have turned to slush. "What about Dale?" I whisper.

Shhh. "Let's listen," Junior says, low.

The room's real uncomfortable, like all the air's blown away. No one says a word; the music's too loud, and folks are rubbernecking between the ironed-shirt guys and the mountain men who are frozen right inside the doorway.

When one of the feds takes a long swig of his Coke, things go back to normal like magic. The two mountain guys leave the door, mosey over to the bar, and sit down.

"So what about this raid, Declan?" Mr. McCord asks the huge man trying to get comfortable on the barstool next to him.

"Well," he says, arranging his tight overalls to make room for his oversized butt, "I hear tell they got that Hicks guy; held him at gunpoint and took him away, siren and lights blarin' all over yonder. Rustled up a bunch of other guys too. Only one I know is Lane Christie from over Cooter's way. Got some woman too; don't know who the hell she is."

Mr. McCord rearranges his baseball cap. "Sounds like they was going after the organizers more than folks doing the betting."

"Got that right. Not so much the betting folks, this time, anyway. I reckon it's a warning to anybody who wants to organize them fights again."

Junior shoves his chair from our table. "Back in a minute."

"Hey, Mr. McCord. Evening, sir," he says to the two men sitting at the bar.

"How you, Junior? Ready for the season to begin?"

"Ready as I'll ever be, I suppose."

"Wish I was your age again," the mountain man says. "Reckon I'd tear up that field."

Junior smiles. "Expect you would, sir. Uh, seems everybody in here's talking about the raid. I happen to know that Hicks guy's real tight with Dale Woodbine. Was he up there, by any chance? Or got caught?"

"Can't say as I know," the man called Declan answers. "Ole Dale, he's sure an ornery one, I'll give him that." He sticks a finger in his beer, messes with the foam, then licks it off. "I'd likely say negative to your question, son. I'd a heard if he got himself tangled in that snare, with his reputation and all."

Junior nods. "Thought that might be the case; just asking. Well, you gents have a real good rest of the evening, hear?"

"You, too, son," Mr. McCord says.

Junie sits back down and puts a look on me. We don't say a word; there's nothing to say.

Jewel's ice clinks in her glass as she puts it down. "Well, I'm real relieved Rucker's not gonna be back for a long time. Got so he scared the bejesus out of me, gunning for y'all. I told him it was Dale's fight, and he had no call to get involved, but he wouldn't listen; just smacked me upside the head a few times, so I shut my mouth."

I look at her kind of hard. "Did he do that often?"

Jewel scrunches up her face, then looks away from me. "Not often, but enough." She shivers, and I put my hand on her arm. She raises her head, stares me in the eyes, and places her hand on mine. We smile at each other, and a surge of happiness for her escape rushes through me. *You're gonna be okay, Jewel. And with half a chance, we'll all be.*

MY PHONE RINGS AT FIVE-ELEVEN. I rub my eyes and squint at the window. It's still dark as the devil's heart outside. "Hey, Junior, what's going on? They get Dale after all?"

"I wish. Naw, Jake just got home. He was up at the fights but stayed pretty much in the shadows, thinking a raid would happen. He said state troopers and FBI guys were everywhere in all directions, and the fight handlers didn't know what hit them. But here's the big news. If it's not just gossip. Word is Sheriff Fletcher was right in the middle of the planning and all. He protected the syndicate and got a cut for letting the fights happen. Maybe he'll finally get arrested."

"Can't be soon enough, you ask me. That guy's a jerk, not to mention a crook who's maybe gonna get his."

"Yeah, let's hope. Anyway, how're you doing with them not catching Dale? You seemed pretty bummed out last night. Hell, I was too."

"I couldn't sleep for worrying on what to do now but never came up with a plan. You think of something, Junie?"

"I keep wondering about where he goes, what he likes, that kind of stuff. He ever tell you anything about his life?"

"I don't know a thing except he uses the dump; suits him real good."

He chuckles at that one. "You recall how we talked in English class last year about brainstorming? We should try it maybe," he says, before letting me answer.

I nod, then realize how dumb that is on the phone. "Okay, what's your schedule today? This is my day off."

"Mine too. Hell, I can meet up at the café soon as you get there. Daddy had me chasing a coyote trying to get our sheep an hour ago."

"Great. I mean, too bad about the coyote but meet you at The Back Door soon as we can get there."

Victory whimpers down the end of my bed. "Hey, girl, how about going for a ride with me?"

Jessie shifts her weight in the other bed. "What the heck's going on?" she says in a scratchy morning voice.

"Nothing. Go on back to sleep; just meeting Junior for breakfast. I'm taking Victory along, so don't be worried about her."

"Okay. Tell Junior hey."

"Sure thing, sis."

The puppy and I head for the kitchen. "C'mon, eat your breakfast. I'm gonna take your water carrier, too, and I better write Mama a note. She'll freak out if she thinks for a second you're gone. Never thought she'd get so attached to you, pup."

When I turn onto Main Street about twenty minutes later, everything's still pretty much deserted. One cop car cruises by slow as sludge, and the local homeless guy's already walking the streets, like he does the whole day long.

Parking my truck in front of the hash-house, I unbuckle Victory. "Okay, baby. Finish your snooze, and I'll be along directly." It's still cool enough that I can leave her with the windows cracked. I check the locks twice, saunter in, and choose a booth.

The only place open before six in Bucktown is The Back Door Café. There's no figuring the folks who own it, though, because there isn't a back door, only a front and side. It's grimy and dark, with a rancid smell; the coffee's okay but nothing else is. An old guy with hair that looks like he slicked it back from the cooking grease can clomps over. I swear he's got a real pirate peg leg. "What can I get you for?"

"Uh, cup of coffee, black and… how are your donuts? I never had any here."

The waiter wipes a filthy looking rag all over the table, spreading more crumbs than before. "Miss, don't nobody have to ask that question at The Back Door. All's we got's quality, and that goes for donuts too."

"Okay, then. I'll have a cake donut with vanilla icing."

The door opens, and the happiest sight in the Ozarks walks in. Junior, with his usual grin strolls over to the table. "You actually gonna eat that donut?" he says, real low. "They make 'em here, you know. I only had one, and it tasted like fish from the Friday night fry-up."

"You have to order more than just coffee in this place, Junior, or they'll throw you out. Just get one, and you can mess around without eating it."

He orders his coffee and donut from the pirate, then paws through his pocket and brings out a chewed pen and piece of spiral notebook paper with the frayed edge still attached, reminding me again that school's coming soon. "Okay, let's brainstorm about Jerk-off."

Holding up my fingers, I start to count. "Well, Dale, for starters, has a mama fixation. He's a major bully and gets off on scaring the hell out of folks. He could have lots of backup with those four brothers. He has no regard for dogs, maybe all helpless animals. And that goes for people too. And he probably sets fires."

Junior glances up from his paper. "Think so?"

I shrug. "Don't know, but he's vicious enough."

Junior writes fast as I talk, then flings down the pen. "He hunts, but so does everybody else in these parts. Seems his best bud is Rucker, so now he'll have to find a new one."

"Here you are, kid," the pirate-waiter interrupts, almost jostling coffee out of the glass pot. "You want more java, girlie?"

I put my hand over the cup. "No thanks." I figure one cup at this dive won't hurt me; I'm not taking a chance with two.

When the guy goes back to the counter, Junie and I look at each other, and I shake my head. "Not much to go on. We gotta locate where he hangs and what he does with his time."

Junior rubs his head. "Do we know anybody who knows him? Jewel, because of Rucker?"

"I don't want to get her involved *at all* now she's away from that creep."

We stare at each other, and I shake my head. Then the tiniest scrap of excitement tickles my insides.

"What're you thinking, Vi? I know that look."

Leaning my elbows on the table, I say, low as low, "The shadow kennel."

"Goddamn if you ain't right!" He ducks his head and glances around. "That's why he wasn't at the fights. He was too busy protecting the cream of the new dog crop. But where is it?"

"Hiding in plain sight, like they say, Junior. Hiding in plain sight."

"Whadda you mean?"

"When you told us about shadow kennels, you said they have to look like the real deal. Like where you buy dogs, you know, to fool the feds and all."

Junior rubs his chin. "Yeah, but we can't go 'round searching for dogs to buy. It'll raise red flags here to Hog Back."

"You're right."

It's weird, but within a second, the world's heavy on my shoulders. I think Junior feels it too. He rests his head on his hands, giant arms propped on the table, and his eyes focused on nothing.

I stare at an antique poster of a grinning blonde girl with pigtails who's digging into a banana split. "It's strange, though. These dogs aren't baying like hounds."

"What? What'd you say?" Junior has a confused look in his eyes, as confused as my mind is, sorting out the jumble in my head.

"Something Doc said. The shadow kennel. I... I have a hunch where it might be."

"HERE'S YOUR HAT; WHAT'S YOUR hurry?" the pirate asks, as we rush to pay the bill. Fumbling, I drop my change all over the floor, then throw Junior my keys. "Would you get Victory out of the truck, and put her in yours?"

"Sure thing," he says, catching them.

I scramble to pick up the coins. It's the guy's tip, and I don't want him to think I threw it on the floor because of horrible donuts and cold coffee.

Jumping into Junior's truck, I look in the backseat. Victory's all belted in and ready to go. "Thanks, Junie," I say, "for taking care of her."

"No problem. She's one great dog."

He noses out onto Main Street and heads toward the Ferguson farm.

I point to my truck. "Think it'll be okay parked in front of The Back Door all day?"

"Sure. Probably the safest place, out in the open like that."

Junior's quieter than usual on our "wild goose chase," as he called it. "You sure it was close to the Ferguson farm where y'all heard the dogs barking?"

"For sure, Junie. I was with Doc on the way out to visit his horse, Barley, that day. And we both heard them."

"Okay, then. We'll do some snooping around."

With the sun full up now, it's going to be a scorcher. Heat's already bouncing off the narrow asphalt road, and leaves are scarce moving on trees as we drive along.

When we get close to the Ferguson farm, Junior seems to change his mind. "I don't know, Vi. You got a longshot going on out here. I mean, you and Doc heard some dogs barking. That's what dogs do in the country; it's their job. Isn't that right, Victory?" he says, glancing at the pup through his rearview mirror.

"Yeah, but even *Doc* thought it was weird, all those dogs barking like that. Usually, only a *passel* of hounds bays, because they're used in the country to hunt. Farmers don't keep bunches of regular dogs on their farms. Too expensive. They generally keep one or two at most to guard their sheep, and chickens, and the like."

"True enough."

"Here, take this country lane, Junie," I say, pointing off to the left.

He slows down, glances in the rearview mirror, and makes a swing onto the little ribbon of rocks that passes for a road. The usually near-dry creek running alongside has water in it from the couple of gully-washers we've had lately. Thickets have knitted together like the nubby sweaters Grandma makes, and horse grass grows in clumps tall as my head.

"Surely is pretty out here, isn't it?" I say. "I'm gonna miss seeing all this when I leave these parts, Junie."

He doesn't answer me, just rubs the top of his head.

The truck stirs up all manner of insects. Yellow butterflies flutter around us, and I hope we don't hit any of them. I want to tell Junie to be careful but don't. He thinks I'm tough inside, but I'm more like one of those butterflies, easy to shatter with a hateful look or harsh word.

"You hear that?" I say, all thoughts of butterflies floating away. I open my window a pinch and can just make out faint barking.

Junior cracks his knuckles on his chin. "Yeah, I do."

Victory gives a low growl from the backseat. "Okay, girl. Nothing for you to worry about." She puts another grumble on me, then quiets down.

"You packin' today, Junie?"

"Naw. Hadn't planned on coming up Hog Back, or I would be. I *did* bring Maw's binoculars, the ones she uses for watching birds. Reckon I'll go have a look-see first and leave the keys here. No point in putting all three of us in danger."

I shake my head real firm. *Huh-uh.* "I'm going too. It's still cool enough this early to leave Victory in the shade. We'll put a couple windows partly down and not be gone long, okay?"

Junior gives me a *What's the use?* shrug. Gravel crunches when he swings the truck around. He maneuvers it over a culvert, then drives straight toward the woods. "Whaddya think? This close to where we heard the noise?"

"Pretty much. Look. There's a protected stand of trees; nice and shady for Victory."

"Okay, then." The truck jostles over roots until we're in the middle of the trees. "You ready?"

My stomach turns over. "Much as I'll ever be, I suppose."

Junior kills the engine, checks his wallet, and grabs the binoculars. He opens his door and shuts it real gentle behind him.

I scoot out, open the back door, and unbuckle Victory. "There, girl. Now you can move around. We won't be long, and you'll be cool enough with the windows cracked a mite." I shut her door easy too. Don't want to make any noise.

"Gotta get my bearings in these woods, Junior," I say. "I'm reckoning the Ferguson farm's about a mile or so to the east." A soft southern breeze plays with my hair, and I could almost forget the reason why we're out here.

"We should hike in a perimeter instead of going straight into that deeper part of the piney forest," he whispers. "Safer that way."

I stop walking and cock my head. "Listen. Hear anything?"

"Yeah, something over to the right. But remember, sound does weird things in deep woods like these. No telling how far or close we are to the dogs, if that's what's making it."

The trees thin out, giving way to rows of thorn bushes. Dense and thick, they may be awesome for rabbits and such, but not so good for me. "Aw, Junie. Snagged my shirt on these brambles. Ripped it. Think there's any other way to go except through these bushes? I'm getting torn to pieces, and the mosquitoes are thick as Dale Woodbine's brain."

"Just be sure you slap 'em quiet as you can."

"Damn if this isn't tick territory too. Don't feel comfortable at all."

"Gotta stop talking, Vi. We could be getting too close."

"Hey, look. I think the track's finally opening up ahead, like into all those black locust saplings. Let's watch those thorns too."

He gives me a thumbs-up, then whispers, "*Quiet* now, hear?"

I cover my mouth and plow on to get away from mosquitoes, and ticks, and anything else that crawls and bites.

"Wait, Vi. Take a gander at what's ahead. A clearing of some sort, definitely manmade. Could be the kennel. Crouch down and go slow. Stay behind me."

Something slams with a *chunk*, like wood on wood. A puppy, a young'un, is crying his heart out like he just lost his mama. My stomach goes all queasy.

Junior treads light-footed and peeks around a couple bushes. "Well, look what we got," he whispers hoarsely. "You call these proper cages for any animal to be in? See 'em stacked up on top of each other? And that so-called roof ain't big enough to keep off sun, rain, or snow."

"Maybe it's to make the dogs meaner, like you said about their treatment, Junie. Uh, you sure nobody's around? This is scaring me something fierce."

"None that I can see. I'm thinking it's only you and me."

The dogs have gone quiet, like they're afraid of barking around people. That thought's not far from the truth.

An open forty-pound sack of dog kibble is lying on the ground like somebody just used it. "Hey, Junie, here's that same off-brand dog food I saw piled up in Dale's truck at Doc's."

"Oh, yeah? And look over there. Nothing like storing it in a tumble-down outbuilding that'll draw rats. These guys are real smart, Vi."

"Listen. That pitiful crying's started up again. Definitely a distressed dog, but where is it?"

"Sound's coming from that direction," Junior says, pointing to some stacked crates. He treads quiet as possible over the pine needles, then stops. "Come on over here, but get prepared."

My hand flies to my mouth, and I hope I don't hurl. A young puppy, mostly black with a few white markings, looks like it's near death. Its neck is rubbed raw and bleeding from a tight metal chain gouging into it. "Little guy's no more'n four months old, tops. With that thing around its neck, he can hardly pick up his head. Why?" My heart's ripping in two.

"Probably being punished for going in its crate's my notion."

"Well, I'm gonna rescue this poor little thing right now."

"Vi, think on it a minute. They're gonna know—"

I bend down, trying to prize apart the links that hold this hateful chain together. *Ughh.* "Give me a hand, will you?"

Junior sighs, stoops over, and pulls the links apart like they're paper. The puppy staggers and tries to stand. I scoop it into my arms. "Aw, you're a little boy. C'mon, let's go while we can."

"We need to take a final check around the kennel area, then get the hell out of here," Junior whispers. "Damn. I left my phone in the car; no signal to speak of out here. But I could still take some pictures. You bring yours?"

I shake my head. "No, left it in the truck for the same reason."

"Well, then, let's head on back to the truck before the devil returns to this hellhole. We gotta figure out how to rescue these dogs real quick. With that pup gone, they'll disappear someplace where they'll never be found."

The puppy snuggles into my arms and gets quiet. Either he senses he may be safe or is worn out from trauma. I'm suspecting trauma wins.

Junior takes the lead, but looks back toward the kennel from time to time. "We'll skirt around those thorn bushes on account of the pup, but it'll take a tad longer."

"Thanks, Junie. I appreciate it."

"Hmph," he says, like always when he knows he's made me happy. "Knew you would."

The rhythm of steady walking has put the puppy to sleep. I clutch him tighter, hoping he'll realize that finally, the misery that was his world is forever over.

33

"WE GOTTA BE ABOUT BACK," Junior says, lifting a huge stem of bindweed that's wrapped itself all around a buckeye tree.

I duck underneath it. "Thanks. Yeah. Feels like the truck's not far—over there, around that stand of pawpaw trees."

"You're right, Vi. I recall seeing them on the way in, wishing we could get us some of that fruit. Not ripe enough yet, though."

"No," I say. "And even if it was, we got no time for that now, things being what they are."

Soon as we trek around the pawpaws, Junior's truck comes into view.

"There it is, Junie. Now I need to stroke this puppy everywhere to get my smell all over him, on Victory's account. Doc warned that you gotta be mindful about bringing in a new dog, and this is a good way to do it."

"Yeah," he says, absentmindedly, and I can tell he's worried about what he could find at the truck. He trudges around the vehicle, then pushes back his St. Louis Cardinals cap. "Don't think anybody's been here, Vi; no vandalism far as I can see."

"That's a relief. Now let's get this baby some of Victory's water, quick."

The puppy's eyes are shut tight, and he feels light and relaxed in my arms. "Hate to wake you up, but how about a drink, little one? You really need it."

Junior snags Victory's plastic jug from the truck and pours water into the container.

I roll the puppy over and stand him on his feet in front of it. He wobbles a mite, sniffs at the water, and starts to drink.

"Look at that, Vi. He's lapping it up like it's his first water ever. These people ain't even people."

"Makes me sick. But the good news is, Mr. and Mrs. Ferguson will be happy with this young'un."

He looks at the pup in a longing way. "Oh, yeah. I'm glad that's where he's going. Now, let's get outta here," he says, sliding into the driver's seat. "We'll get this little guy to the Fergusons first thing and—damn! Damn, Vi. I lost my wallet! It's not in my pocket!"

"What? No, you couldn't have."

"Well, I surely did; must a dropped it back there." He slams the steering wheel. Hard. "Goddamn it to hell!" His shoulders slump. "I gotta go back. It can't stay there, not with a pup gone. They'll come gunnin' for us both before this day's over."

I know he's right, and it's all my fault, me taking the puppy. "I'm going with you."

"No."

"Yes. Two searching's gonna cut the time in half."

He sighs but doesn't say anything more.

I look down at the tiny dog on my lap, and a flutter of fear touches my heart. "We need to put the puppy in next to Victory and watch her close for a minute. I'm thinking she'll be fine with him while we're gone, just want to be sure."

"Look, Vi…" Junior starts.

I shake my head. "Nothing else to say, except let's put these two pups together, check out Victory's behavior, and go find the wallet."

My heart starts to pound when I put the puppy next to Victory. She sniffs him everywhere and shifts her gaze hard at me. "Good girl. Good girl," I coo and stroke her head. She stares at the pup and back at me, then starts licking him with her long tongue. "Good girl, good girl," I say over and over.

"I'm pretty content with her reaction to the pup. What do you think, Junie?"

"Heck if I know. You're the vet, Vi. You say so, it's good enough for me."

"Okay, then. Let's get this hunt over with fast."

He closes the back door soft, so the latch hardly catches.

I grab my phone and do the same with mine.

Junie and me, we're spare of words trudging back to the kennel. I'm figuring we're both pretty much thinking the same thoughts about danger, and Dale, and the need to be quick-witted. When we reach those bramble bushes, I don't fret one time about tearing my clothes; only thing worrying me is a close encounter with crazy Dale.

With Junior in the lead, I try to concentrate on both sides of us while keeping an eye to the ground for the lost wallet. Problem is, my mind wants to wander back to the two dogs, and I'm hoping real hard that Victory's minding that baby good.

Junior whirls around to face me. "Down, Vi!" He hits the ground like a soldier on a battlefield.

I fall to the forest floor and force my face to the ground. The loamy soil smell panics me. *Ticks!* There gotta be millions of them around here. The need to pick my face up off these pine needles takes my breath away, but I can't 'cause what I see through the bushes makes ticks unimportant. It's Dale. About thirty yards ahead of us. His rifle's ready for business, and a sheathed knife is around each leg. A shift in his stance, a kind of a crouch like a lion ready to pounce, tells me he heard something.

"All right, whoever you are," he half-yells in a slow, low voice, "y'all might as well come on out from wherever you're hiding. Guaranteed I'll find you, and wasting my time's gonna make me madder than I am now."

Dale must not have found the wallet, or he'd be ranting about it. Gotta stay still, still as death. A wood tick thumps along, right at eye level. My hand flies to my mouth. *Don't scream.* Ticks jump on their prey, and I'm it. That bloodsucker's gone. Where'd it go? Pounced on me. *Eww.* I swipe at my face. "Get off me!"

"What're you farting around here for? Well, I tell you what; this is my lucky day. Yours? Not so much, 'cause you ain't getting out of here alive. Stand up!"

I shuffle to my feet, aware that Junior's hidden behind a thick nettle bush a little ahead of me. Can't look toward him; dead giveaway.

"Now, I'll ask again, real polite. What're you doing in these woods?"

"I'm searching for a good tree," I say, hoping my shaky voice sounds as mean as his. "Got me a new stand. Since you're the expert, Dale, how about some suggestions?"

A snaky smile turns him into more of a monster than he already is. "Girlie, listen to that mouth on you. Y'all oughta be thankin' me. Hell, I put some backbone into your scrawny body. Not long ago, you was quaking when you laid eyes on me. Now you see me, you're full of sass. All's I got to say is, enjoy it long as you can, if you catch my drift."

I stare at the monster.

"Well," he continues, "I've waited for this day ever since my maw was carried on home."

"Sorry for your loss." *Why am I so stupid*?

"Sorry? What you sorry about? You're cut from the same cloth as your no-account maw. You got no *sorry* feelings in you." He hawks and spits a clot of tobacco juice toward the bush where Junior's hiding. "My maw, she... she was the best woman ever stepped foot on this earth. Go on. Ask anybody."

"Dale, I only found out about our mamas a little bit ago, and I was real upset too. But killing me and *my* mama isn't the answer."

He fills his lungs and screams, "What *is* the answer then!" Aiming his rifle heavenward, he plugs the sky with two rounds. Dogs bark and birds rise out of nowhere in a flurry of wings. Dale blubbers and wipes his nose with the back of his hand; snot streams everywhere. Fear pierces my heart like a honed hunting knife. He's crazy dangerous, and this is as bad as it gets.

Dale grabs hold of his filthy shirt like he's gonna tear it to pieces. "When my maw was dying, did she call out for Daddy or any of us brothers? No! Over and over, she cried for Cora. 'I need Cora.

Bring me Cora. I can't go to Jesus without seeing Cora.'" He spits on the ground for emphasis, I suppose.

"Look, Dale—"

"Shut your gob. You wanted to know why you're getting dead. Well, I'm obliging you."

He lowers his head, then lifts it slow as treacle syrup stirs. Squinting, he licks his lips, and I know he can't wait to say what he's fixing to say. "When we found out about your maw always sniffing after ours, we went gunning those years back. But our maw, she begged us not to kill Cora, so we took care of your paw instead. I slammed two bullets in him; made sure he didn't wake up."

Terror! Every nerve in my body is screaming to run, but can I? *Eyeball everything. Be aware.* There's a truck with no key behind me, open meadow ahead, woods to my right, Junior's thicket to my left. Not much to work with.

"Hey, you listening to me?" Dale hollers. "I'm not flapping my gums for nothing here. No, just trying to be *po*-lite before I send you to harp land."

"Yeah, my ears are tuned directly your way so I won't miss a thing."

Crazy Dale scratches his head with the gun barrel end. He sets a bug-eyed stare on me that's likely full of meth and definitely plain old wickedness. I quake so bad, I can scarce control any muscle in my body.

"Well," he continues, "with your paw gone, that was the end of our troubles with your maw, or so we thought. But we was wrong, dead wrong, turns out." He spews tobacco filth toward Junior's bush again, and I surely hope he hasn't figured him to be there.

"Come a time the cancer put itself heavy on Maw and wouldn't let loose." He stomps back and forth and waves his gun all over the place. "After Maw's ruckus about Cora, Daddy sent for her, 'cause by then my maw, she was dyin' real hard. It was your maw put the cancer on her. Makin' my maw do… unnatural stuff. Ruined her body's what it did."

He's gone 'round the bend, and there's no coming back.

"When Cora walked into Maw and Daddy's bedroom, she fell on my maw, and we couldn't hardly prize her off. Cora said it was part of the treatment, like the slobbery kisses she put all over Maw's face, but she didn't fool Daddy none. And that's when he told us the *whole* story about… what was *really* going on for all those years. Cora… tainted her; turned her away from bein' normal. And that's why you're going to die, here, today. My maw won't be set free to angel fly till you and your maw are cold in the ground."

Dale wipes his nose with the back of a hand again, then covers his eyes and cries like a baby.

This is my chance, but I don't know what to do with it.

I back up slow, with my eyes nailed to his. He fumbles around in his jeans pocket for what I hope's a handkerchief, finds it, wipes his face, then sets the same beady gaze on me. "Don't think about running. I'll plug you in the back soon as look at you." He raises his gun and hollers, "This here's for my maw, my daddy, and my brothers. I hope you're watching from up yonder, Maw."

I stretch my arm out. "Dale! Don't!"

"Right here, creep!" Junior charges forward like Dale's the end zone. Head down, hands clenched, straight toward the goal, he's a machine at full power.

"What the hell?" In one motion, Dale aims his gun and shoots. Junior crumples into a heap and doesn't move.

"No! Junior!" I start running toward him, but Dale catches me around the shoulders. He jerks me around to face him.

My eyes fill with fire. "You bastard! You crazy bastard."

Flecks of spit cover Dale's mouth. He swipes it with the back of his hand then flings his rifle to the ground "I'll show you who's crazy."

Thrashing around, I punch at him best I can. Only get in one good shin-kick when he slams me to the forest floor, then puts a look on me that pretty near stops my heart. Ham hands close around my windpipe. Throat's Dale-squeezed. Fingers turn to claws, prizing his pincers away. No use. No good. I'm dying here on this forest floor. My eyes roll up and meet blue sky. World's got quiet; can't hardly see a thing.

Then, like a miracle, his death grip on my neck loosens, and his hands sort of shimmy down my neck and stop at my collarbone. "Bear! Bear's got my leg! I'm bear bit! Help me. You hear? Somebody help me!"

Dale's screams turn my blood to ice. Sweat streams thick down my face, like rain of a summer's night. And I hear them. Growls, low growls, vicious growls that won't stop. *That pathetic cop was right. There are bears around here.*

Old Dale must be dead—or wounded bad. He's not moving a hair. But in case he isn't, I gotta get away from him. And before the bear has a chance to get me. *Roll away. Roll away.*

My head's pounding, vision's blurry. Got the shakes so hard I can't stop biting my lip. I force my eyes to open. No bear. There's no bear. Too small. Looks like a dog. Like Victory! She has Dale around the throat and is growling, frightful as a grizzly. "Good girl, good girl," I croak.

Crawling back over to Dale, I pull his knives from their sheaths, check up and down his leg for more weapons, then scoot away quick. He's still lying real quiet, but I can tell he's alive. Dead people don't have sweat pour down their faces or clench and unclench their fists like they want to move, but know they better not if they want to see another sunrise.

I stagger to my feet, slow, but keep a close watch on his fists. I cough, then clear my throat. "What's gonna happen to you is mainly for my daddy who you put in an early grave, you yellow-belly pitiful excuse of a human. Now I'm getting Junie some help."

Someone answers on the first ring. "Nine-one-one. What's your emergency?"

"Help. Need help. Friend shot. Chest. Please. Come. Fast."

"Yes, ma'am," a distant voice says. "I got your location. Help's on the way. Stay on the phone."

"Thanks. I'm goin' nowhere. Not without Junior."

It's impossible to see Junie around those thickets, and I can't leave Dale to check.

"Junior, Junie, help's coming," I holler over and over, loud as my voice will let me. "Please be alive."

Way before I see them, I hear vehicles thunder up the lane, sirens screaming. Two squad cars and an ambulance kick up a trail of gravel dust, then screech to a stop at the tree line. "Stay, Victory," I say, putting my hand close to her nose. Dale looks up at me, eyes pleading. Mine don't answer.

"GET BACK, MISS," THE LADY medic from the ambulance says. "We need room to work."

"Okay. Sorry."

She gives me a concerned look. "I know you're worried, but we're doing everything we can to help him."

"Yes, ma'am, and I appreciate it, so much."

I try hard not to cry, but it's no use.

"Junie. You're getting help right now." Sitting on the pine needles with Victory next to me, I stroke Junior's hand, then hold it tight. His eyes kind of flicker at my touch, and I'm grateful for that tiny trickle of hope.

The medic takes his blood pressure, then starts an IV. "Stay with me, son," she says, cutting the front of his shirt.

"Is he going to die?"

She checks that the drip's flowing, then looks at me with hard pity, and that scares the bejesus out of me. "Too soon to know. I need to find out where all he's shot."

A policeman walks over and squats down. "Now, I want to ask you again, miss. Are you sure you're okay? We're finished with all the photos we need of your neck and arms and the crime scene, but we want to be satisfied that you are... otherwise unharmed."

"No. I promise. My dog rescued me before that creep could..." I force back a sob. "She saved my life. I want him to go away for a long time and wouldn't do anything to stop it."

"Well, you don't have to worry about that," he says. "Attempted murder? He'll be too old to do damage by the time he sees his life without bars in front of it."

"Good," I say in a fierce whisper. "And, Officer? Thank you, kindly."

He squeezes my shoulder real gentle, stands up, and walks back to his squad car.

I look back at Junie. *If only they can save your life, I'll be grateful for the rest of mine.*

34

THE SURGERY WAITING ROOM'S EMPTY except for me. Why did Junior's folks choose today visit his great-granny up in Quincy? They still got an hour's drive.

People have come and gone, some smiling and some crying after talking to the doctor. The wall clock says it's ten minutes later than last time I looked, which makes it three twenty-three p.m. Junior's been in surgery for four hours. His wounds must be terrible bad to take this much time.

I think back to finding Victory. Her surgery took Doc three hours to complete. *There's not too much difference treating dogs, or cows, or people. You'll realize that more clearly when you're in vet school.*

"Miss Sinclair?"

A tall man with gray hair and a long white coat walks toward me, and the memories of Doc's words float from my mind. I hop up from the table so fast my chair tumbles over. "Oops. Uh, yes. I'm Miss Sinclair. Uh, Violette, that is."

A slight smile from him. My heart kicks upward.

"I'm Dr. Munro, head surgeon of young Mr. McKenna's team. He's out of surgery and is holding his own."

I can't seem to speak.

He picks up the chair and motions for me to sit back down. He sits at the one across from me and props his elbows on the table.

I want to yell at him to tell me how Junie is, but instead I take a deep breath and swallow hard.

He gives me a tired smile. "It was touch and go for a while. The bullet passed through his right lung, which collapsed. That's been successfully repaired, but the blood loss was significant, about thirty percent, close to what a person can lose and still live. We had to remove his spleen, which also causes blood loss, but we were able to transfuse him, keep him from bleeding out."

I still can't speak, so I nod.

The doctor squeezes the back of his neck. "We worked hard on him, and with youth and strength on his side, my opinion is he'll be good as new." This time he offers me a real smile. "Of course, he'll have a scar here and there, but from what I've heard, those'll be badges of courage."

"Thank you, Doctor. He's my best friend and took the bullet for me."

"That's what I understand. You're a lucky young woman. Most people don't have such friends."

"Yes, sir. Thank you again. Is… Can I maybe see him now?"

"Normally I'd say no, but in this instance, I think it'll do him good for you to be there. I'll call the head nurse and make arrangements. Good luck to you both."

Before I can say another word, he stands up and is gone. I stare at the door that closed behind him. *Do I sit down or stand and wait for the nurse?* I almost get my butt back on the chair when the door swishes again. "Miss Sinclair? Come with me, please."

I nod and follow the nurse into Intensive Care. It's cold, and mysterious machines click and whir in tiny rooms full of patients.

"Here we are; Cubicle Nine," she says, letting me go in first.

The little room feels full of power, like it's working hard to keep death away. My Junie's laying on a narrow bed and is still as stone. Many tubes are connected to him, including an oxygen line. But he's breathing, and his cheeks are pink, and he's going to live.

"Hey, Junie." I squeeze his hand, and he squeezes mine back, then tries to open an eye. "No, take it easy. You recollect when I was Dale-beat? You told me that so much it made me crazy." He tries to smile, but it comes out half, and that's good enough for me.

Junior is conscious, and then he isn't. Reminding myself that this is how wounded animals react after surgery, too, should help, but it doesn't so much. His afternoon nurse tells me goodbye, and the evening one introduces himself, then starts all the previous nurse's procedures over again. No one asks me to leave, and I thank Dr. Munro under my breath, 'cause I'm not going, not yet.

I hold Junie's hand and rub his arm until my head gets all heavy, and my mind fuzzes up like it does just before I fall asleep. Some folks are murmuring right inside the door of Intensive Care in my dream. But my body becomes rubber when Mr. and Mrs. McKenna and Jake tiptoe into Cubicle Nine. I rub my eyes, then blink up at them. *What are they gonna say to me?*

Jake walks in the tiny room first and stares at his brother. Mr. and Mrs. McKenna follow him, nod at me, and then hover over their son.

I stand up real wobbly-like and step back to make room for the family. No one says a word while they gaze down at Junie. The only sounds are those coming from machines working hard to keep him alive.

After forever, Jake turns and wraps his arms around me. "Violette, you done good, girl. Dale Woodbine's one crazy mean devil, and he got what he deserved. Why, hell, you and Junior did the whole county a favor. Nobody's gonna forget it, either, if I have any say-so."

A sob closes up my throat, and I work at pushing it back down. "Thanks for those words. They mean an awful lot." I pull away and look him directly in the eye. I think he knows what's coming, but his stare doesn't waver, and that heartens me. "Uh, Jake? The best get-well present you could give Junior is no more cooking and such." Maybe it's the wrong time, but it needed saying. I hold my breath.

He looks me hard in the eyes. "I made a deal with myself on the drive here. I'm gonna try real hard to stop. With my brother doing what he did to save you? Puts me to shame."

"Junior's been out-of-his-head worried for you, so he'll be proud to hear that."

Mrs. McKenna turns around and gives me a weak smile. "Violette, I'm gonna hug your neck. You surely need one after what you've been through."

"Mrs. McKenna," I say, but can't go on. My tears nearly carry me away. "I'm so sorry for all's happened. This wasn't his worry or his fight, and he didn't have to get involved."

She dabs at her eyes with a tissue. "No, but if any of this can help Jake, well, Junior, he'll say it's all been worth the doing. He told me and his paw more than once that trying to catch Dale was worth the doing if Jake could be helped." She puts a look on me that says she's done with blame.

The McKennas, they're strong Ozark folk like us Sinclairs. Spare of words and tough as oak bark, like my grandma says.

Junior's mama brushes away what I know is the last tear in this conversation. "How're you getting home, Violette?"

"Jessie just got her driver's license, so she's picking me up directly. This'll be her first time driving someplace she doesn't know, but she's careful."

Junior's daddy pats my arm. "I know she'll do fine if she's anything like her big sister."

No surprise Junior's so great. With folks like his, how could he not be?

ABOUT AN HOUR LATER, MY phone vibrates. Jessie's headed up to Intensive Care from the lobby.

"I'll mosey on out to the waiting room," Jake says. "Let her say hey to Junior."

I hear a buzzer, and Jessie appears at the entrance to Cubicle Nine. "I'm awful glad to see you, Junior," she says, wiping a spilt tear off his hand. And our mama sends her regards." She glances at Mr. and Mrs. McKenna. "And the same to you too."

"Thank her kindly for that," Junior's daddy says.

Jessie nods and gazes around the tiny room, like she's seeing it for the first time. "Get well fast, you hear? Vi misses you already. And… me too."

"Oh, he squeezed my hand, Vi," she says in a surprised voice.

I nod and smile. "How was your drive here?"

"At least I didn't hit no... anybody. I reckon that's a mercy."

"A mercy's what it is, all right," Mr. McKenna says. "In no time, though? You'll be driving all over creation and thinkin' nothing of it."

Jessie puts a little smile on him. "Thanks, Mr. McKenna. I surely look forward to that time."

"Time to go now, sis," I say.

I give Junie's big hand a light grip. "We'll be back, Junie. You hear? Can't get rid of us."

"Take care of yourselves, girls," Mrs. McKenna says. "And Violette, you get yourself some rest."

"Yes, ma'am," I say.

My sister hugs me hard at the elevator, and I hug her back. "I feel bad about leaving, Jess. I mean, part of me wants to stay, but a bigger part of me wants to go real bad now I know he's gonna be okay. This place is tough; wears a body out. Hope I'm not being weak for Junie."

"Aw, Vi. Hospitals are awful, unless you need one bad. Then they're like sent from heaven. You're just saying what everybody thinks." She pauses and looks me over like Doc's X-ray machine. "You really okay? Sure got a lot of bruises all over."

"Yeah, but I'm alive, and that's something."

"Sure is, Vi. It's been some kind of summer, you ask me. But by God, you got him, and Rucker too."

"Just lucky."

"Yeah. Right. I'd like a little of that luck. You know, the kind you make yourself."

"There's something I can't figure, Jess."

"What?"

"About Dale. Seems like the only goodness he had in life was his mama. I've been thinking on that."

"Don't tell me you're going all soft on him. He's a monster. He tried to kill you! And he *almost* killed Junior."

"I know, but… you think there was *ever* any good in him?"

Jessie looks me hard in the eyes. "I don't have any way to answer that."

"Neither do I, really. Just wondering. Only wondering."

We're quiet walking side by side through the hospital's automatic doors. The night air is warm and velvety, like a cloak that wraps soft around your skin. It's wonderful to be outside, away from tubes, and IVs, and machines that keep you one step from death. "Victory get home all right, Jess? The policeman promised he'd take care of both pups."

"You bet. That guy's your biggest fan. Said you and Junior are heroes; did a huge service to Hitchens County, bringing Dale to justice."

I open my mouth for the next question and Jess interrupts. "Yes, the puppy's home too. He didn't jump out of Junior's truck or anything after Victory pushed the door open. The policeman, Officer McCall? He took him to the Fergusons first. Mrs. Ferguson called home to thank you before I left for here. Said she'll get back in touch directly."

Relief for both dogs' safety rushes through me, so much that I fight back tears. "I'm awful happy about the Fergusons and that puppy."

When we get in the car, Jessie looks long at me. "Mama's on the warpath, Vi."

I buckle my seatbelt. "Now what?"

"She found that letter you have, and she's on a rip. Wouldn't tell me what was in it, and I pretended I didn't know."

"You mean she went through my stuff? I had that hidden in my chifforobe."

"Mama said it was on the floor *next* to your chifforobe. I don't know, Vi. I really don't. Mama, she's acting peculiar, more than she does usually."

"What do you mean?"

"She... she's sort of... living in her head." Jess nods. "Yeah, that's it. But at least you won't have to deal with her tonight. She'll be in bed by the time we get home."

I look across the seat. "You want me to drive?"

"Nuh-uh. I'm gonna be like you and just do it."

35

JESSIE AND I ARE AWAKE at first light. "Can I get in bed with you like I used to when I was little, Vi?"

"You don't ever have to ask, sis. You're thinking about Mama too?"

"Yeah. Want me there when you talk to her about... what you gotta say?"

"Naw, but thanks. Mama and me? We gotta go it alone on this one."

"I understand. Just... just want you to know I'm here. If you need me."

"I know that, Jess. And I'll know it the rest of my life. And I love you and thank you for being such a good sister."

"Me, too, Vi. Me too. About you."

We hold onto each other tight and watch first light filter through our window.

* * *

EVERYTHING IS BEAUTIFUL, AND FRESH, and clean to me this morning when I step outside, ready to go to work. Speaking of mercies, they're thick on the ground today. I didn't have to face Mama, for one thing. I snag a mug of coffee, gulp it down, and sprint to my truck. Not quite up to a Mama-meet-up first thing; better let it wait for later, when both our heads are clearer and our hearts are steadier. I smile at the sky; same one I was saying goodbye to yesterday. But one day later, old Dale's behind bars with Rucker, where they belong, and Junie's on the mend.

When I reach Bucktown, nothing looks as down-at-the-heels as it usually does. The same folks are on Main Street, doing the same things, but I reckon I'm seeing it through different eyes— maybe for the first time. The policeman who's always patrolling in his car this time of day actually salutes me when he passes. *Could I be dreaming?*

I swing into the clinic parking lot and pull into my usual spot. A pang hits my heart when I think about Junior's truck here that morning a few weeks back and how happy I was to see it. *Come on, Vi. Don't dwell on the past. You and Junie have a whole future to look forward to.*

I step out of the truck, take a deep breath of good old Ozark air, and walk on into the clinic. *What the heck's going on?* Loud clapping's coming from pet owners, and Loretta, and Doc. "No, stop," I mutter.

"Stop nothing," Loretta shouts. "What you and Junior did for this county's nothing short of a miracle, Violette Sinclair. Word's out all over these hills, and nobody's gonna forget it."

Doc hugs me real strong. "But don't scare us like this anymore, okay?"

"Okay."

I give her a smile, but it's only my outside smile. Inside I'm laughing all over; a busting-out, biggest laugh ever. I am so... happy. But when the phone rings, my heart kicks me in the chest so hard I can scarce breathe. *Who's calling me? Doesn't matter. The bad guys are gone. Unless it's terrible news about Junie.*

"Hello?" I ask, my voice shaking.

"Violette?"

"Yes," I say, still sort of wary.

"This is Mrs. McKenna. Somebody wants to tell you hi."

"Junie?"

"Hey," says a weak, sandpapery voice.

"I... it's so good to hear your voice."

"You too," he whispers.

"I'll be over to see you soon, Junie."

"Yeah, goin' home... few days. Movin' me out of Intensive today."

"Great! You'll be able to rest better outta there."

Funny, 'cause much as I care for Junie, I'm finding words hard to say, and I hate myself for it.

"Vi?"

"Yeah, Junie."

"Promise me something?"

"Anything," I say.

"Stay outta trouble... till I get home."

"Promise. I... love you, Junie."

"Love you too, Vi."

36

Mama's car isn't parked in her spot this afternoon, and I'm not surprised, what with the unfinished business between us. I trudge across the yard and up the porch steps. "Hey, Jess, you and Victory look awful comfortable out here. She's taken to you so much. She won't leave *your* side, either."

Jess puts a kiss on her forehead. "I love her too."

"Looks like the Fergusons got you home from your puppy visit."

"They were so nice to let me play with him, Vi. He's the cutest thing, and isn't Elvis the best name for him?" Without letting me answer, she says, "He wants to sit on their laps all the time when he's not exploring."

"He's gonna be a great part of their family."

"Uh, Vi. Speaking of family, you get a chance to talk to Mama yet? Like on the phone or anything?"

"No. I suppose we're both making ourselves scarce just now, with that letter and all."

Jessie pops a piece of purple bubble gum in her mouth. "Yeah, I get that. Well, I gotta fill out this Discount Dollar application form. Maybe I'm not gonna like being sixteen that much."

"Need any help?"

"Naw. Think I can manage it, Vi, but thanks."

I clap my hands at Victory. "Hey, how about a walk?" She scrambles down the steps fast as a pig to pudding, then tears on over to the woods, nose to the ground, snuffling wild scents.

Crunching across baked grass, I think about the fall rains that'll be coming soon, turning everything back to green till a killing frost lies thick on the ground. After this summer, I'm ready for it.

"There's the tree, girl. Looks like Uncle Gray took that stand down today, just like he said he would."

It's weird, but I'm not scared anymore. Maybe Dale was right about him giving me a backbone. Talk about life being downright crazy.

Something *plops* behind me, and Victory grumbles at it. "Acorns falling already, puppy. Gonna be an early autumn. School's coming on fast, Victory. Junior and me, we'll have one more year together before college."

My dog and I loop around the south woods, stop to play fetch with a stick, then head for home. Mama's car's back. My heart's not ready for what we have to say to each other. And even with all that's happened, I may hate what she does, but Lord help me, I love her.

"Victory, let's be quiet going in." But she hurtles into the kitchen for a drink of water. Mama's sure to be there, so I follow her on in.

Leaning over the sink, sinewy arms fiercely scrubbing garden vegetables, Mama's fixing supper like always, no matter what.

I watch her a second. Old habits die hard, my grandma says. What's Mama's gonna do when me and Jess leave? A hollow place carves into my middle, so strong it all but takes my breath away. "I see you're home."

She doesn't turn around. "Yep, not long ago."

My eyes wander around our old-timey kitchen, with its scarred floorboards and its counter cluttered with cook pans and the cast iron skillet Mama's gonna fry chicken in for supper. Great-Granny Sinclair's hickory-wood pie safe is tucked in the corner where it's been all my life.

I should feel secure in this room; maybe not happy, but secure at least. Instead, my heart's about to pound clean out of my chest, my mouth's aquiver, and it's all I can do to keep from running clear outside. "Uh, Mama," I say in a shaky voice, "about that letter."

Her back stiffens, and the dirt-crusted carrot she just picked up from the counter *thunks* into the sink. I know I'll hear that sound my whole life.

"I was wrong to read it and feel... horrible that I did."

Mama's a living statue, waiting, waiting for what's coming next.

"But being's I did... please know I... understand, much as I'm able... and I feel so terrible for you and Mrs. Woodbine—and for Daddy and Mr. Woodbine too."

The two of us are rooted to the kitchen floor as a sweet breeze floats in, stirring our hearts in different ways, I'll wager. She drops her knife into the sink and turns around slow. Deep valleys of darkness lay under her eyes, and her face is a pitiful shade of ghost.

Miss Havisham in *Great Expectations*. I remember the book's title now, but it gives me no pleasure.

Mama raises her head to the breeze, takes a deep breath, and I know our lives will change forever after this minute. "She was me, and I was her. Sweet Jesus forgive me, there was nothing I could do to remedy it."

My stomach churns. *I don't want to hear this.* "Mama, I—"

She holds out her left hand to shush me, the one that carries her gold wedding band. "In Our Lord's eyes, it's a grievous sin that'll follow me to my grave like it did with my poor Hazel."

I know for a surety she loves saying Mrs. Woodbine's name out loud, and sweet Jesus help *me*, I get it.

"I've been a hypocrite and a coward with you, Violette. Gray said that to my face a long time ago when we first... knew about you. I didn't want you to go through the hell I... me and Hazel went through, is all."

"I understand, Mama."

But I'm a liar, because I don't comprehend any of it.

Then Mama, she keens a wail such as I never heard before and hope not to again, and I'm put in mind of Grandma's tales of haints and Ozark Howlers. When she's finished and only sniffles are left, Mama shakes her head like nobody's here, even her. She holds her arms and rubs them hard, and I'd swear she's straining to get the skin off or maybe turn into a different person.

"No, that's *not* all. I been ashamed to have a daughter with my affliction, to watch her tormented... like it turned out you've been. And I did nothing to stop it; my own flesh and blood." She casts a stare on me that'd scare anybody, let alone her daughter.

"I should have stood up for you, and I never did. Gray… Gray, he cautioned me this day would come, and I… I didn't heed…"

The space we're in is silent but for the ticking clock, and the dripping faucet, and the hum of the old fridge motor. Time isn't time anymore, just like when I was Dale-beat. It's stopped and waits; it waits for Mama.

"Our craving for each other never went away. So a week before that Thanksgiving, me and Hazel made plans to start meeting again. All we had to do was find a safe place. I'd already carried myself over to Branson to buy things, pretty things to wear."

Please, Mama. I'm your daughter. I can't listen to any more.

Hiding her eyes behind work-hardened hands, she starts to cry again, but this time soft as the goose-down comforters Grandma makes. "And then your daddy was gunned down. Shot by a Woodbine—Dale, not Walter. The guilt and sorrow near ate me up till there was almost nothing left but… the longing for Hazel. I tried not to love her with all that happened. God knows I tried."

Mama's started gulping in air so hard, I'm afraid she's gonna give herself a heart attack.

"With your daddy dead and gone, and Walter out to murder us, our plans were impossible. Walter and his gang of thugs, including his sons, watched Hazel by day and night. Put her under the threat of death, they did. And me. And you girls. I worried so bad about you and Jessie. That's when I sent y'all packing up to Gray and Zinnie."

I remember.

Mama stands in front of me and looks at nothing. But I know she's been carried back seven years in her mind. "Gray, he went up Hog Back. Had it out with Walter. Zinnie and me, we was scared to death until he came on back down unharmed. Told Walter he'd kill him, and nobody'd ever find his body, if he didn't stop threatening Sinclair women. No matter if they was married into the clan or born of it; made no difference. They were Sinclairs, and Gray would put him in the ground."

Mama makes a rasping sound, like she can't get her breath.

"Can I get you some water?" I ask, not knowing what else to say but needing to say something.

She looks through me like she doesn't know what I'm asking, takes a deep breath and closes her eyes—at the memory of what she's gonna tell me is my guess. "Then Hazel, she was beat horrible by Walter, almost to death. He wouldn't take her to a hospital, and she walked with a limp until the day she died. How they got wind of our plans, they'll take to their graves and there it will stay."

"I'm so sorry, Mama."

I don't think she hears me.

"It didn't stop that cruel Walter from sniffing around, stalking us, trying to catch us like the last time. He hungered to kill us both. To this day I don't know how come I'm still walking the Lord's earth instead of laying in the woods somewhere, a pile of bones never to be found."

She clasps her hand to her heart like some statues you see in Catholic churches. "I'm wicked in Our Lord's eyes, and try as I might, doing good church works and all, they won't help me come Judgment Day."

I want to hug her bony frame but don't dare. She never was one for much touching, from us, anyway. "Mama, listen to me. You're *human*, not wicked. Hear me? Think on those words. Please. Our

Lord says that all who believe will enter the Kingdom of Heaven. *All*, Mama. That surely means you."

She raises her apron hem, blotting eyes that are only sorrow, and I wonder how many jugs of tears have been wiped away by that fabric. Mama looks down and smooths out her apron. "Law, it's getting late. Jess'll be home soon, and supper's scarce started."

She's through, and I know the name Woodbine will never be mentioned again in this house by her. I try my best to smile, but I think it comes out tears.

But when I look full-on at Mama, there's a light in her eyes I haven't seen since I was a little kid, when nobody bullied or made fun of me. "Soon as he's able, we'll have Junior over for supper. It's high time I thanked him for saving your life. But for now, would you mind setting the table… Vi?"

"I'd be happy to, Mama."

I HEAR A CAR, MUFFLER backfiring, pull up behind my truck. It's Jewel bringing Jessie home for supper. Mama and me, we got everything ready, and there's no time to tell Jess what happened.

The front door opens then slams shut. "Hey, y'all. Smells like Sunday afternoon in here. What's goin' on?"

Hurrying to the front room fast as possible, I say, "Mama surprised us with fried chicken tonight. Can you beat that?"

"How come? 'Cause Junior's gonna live?"

"Something like it," I murmur, hoping she'll look directly in my eyes so I can give her a signal. She doesn't, though, and traipses off to the bathroom.

Try as I might, I can't get Jessie alone before supper. Mama's always there, watching us out of the corner of her eye. And for the first time in my life, the notion runs through my head that maybe she's scared of *us*. Of what we might do, or think of her, or act. The thought shocks me. I need to run it by Jess.

Don't you worry none, Mama. Jess and me? We're going to be a lot nicer to you than you've been to us.

37

SUPPER MAKES ME CRY INSIDE. Mama tries so hard to be our old mama. And even though I know it won't be like this all the time, or maybe ever again, it's what Jess and I have yearned for our whole lives.

Mama picks up the empty faded-flowers platter and smiles. "Y'all did a good job with the chicken. Glad you liked it. You girls want a cup of coffee now? After supper, I mean? It's been such a nice time talking and all..."

Jess shakes her head. "I couldn't eat or drink another thing, Mama. What a supper. I love your fried chicken. And it was fun talking like regular... uh, that's not what I meant to say."

I stand up. "We know, sis. Let's clear."

In the kitchen, Jessie opens her eyes wider than anything, puts her palms up, and stares at me.

"Later," I mouth.

My sister gives me a look, but says nothing more.

"Mama, you look tired," Jessie says, picking up the last dishes from the table. "Why don't you go on in the front room, put your feet up. We'll straighten out the kitchen."

She stares at Jess and me like she's laying eyes on us for the first time, and maybe she is. "That's thoughtful, girls. Thank you."

Jessie and me, we don't say a word doing the kitchen cleanup. I know we're each thinking our own thoughts, trying to put together the riddle that is our mama. Jess hangs the wet dishtowel on the oven handle and looks at me. I nod toward the front door, and we head on down the hall to it.

Soon as we settle on the top step of the porch, Jessie whispers, "What in the name of God was all that... niceness about? I think she's got the old age disease or some such, Vi."

"Listen to what happened this afternoon. I've tried to tell you, but Mama's been... in the way."

JESSIE SNIFFLES THE WHOLE TIME I tell her about Mrs. Woodbine, and them meeting, and Mr. Woodbine finding them. "Poor Mama. It's downright... tragic, like the stuff *you* carry on about in Shakespeare or something. Her life's been, well, pitiful."

"Yes, it has, Jess."

My sister rubs hard at her eyes, and I know what's coming. "Only thing is, I feel awful bad about Daddy."

My heart clinches, and I suspect always will, in thinking about Mama and Mrs. Woodbine, and our daddy. "Me, too, Jess. Daddy, he didn't deserve what happened; being married to Mama and all." I shake my head and wipe away my own tears. "But we gotta dwell on the good things. He loved us, and we loved him. Whether he loved Mama or not? Nothing we could do about that, hard as it is to say."

She nods, pulls out what I call *a just-in-case tissue* from her pocket, and blows her nose hard. "Don't you wish we'd been able to meet... Hazel? See what she was like? I do."

I nod. "Yeah, but I bet she was pretty much like most women around here. Be hard to tell her apart from the others. She was special to Mama, though. So special it ruined both of their lives."

"What do you think about Mama treating us nice? That gonna last?"

"Jess, I... don't know. But it surely is fine for the moment."

My sister squirms on the top step, a sure sign something important is coming. "Do you... do you think when you're finished with college and vet school... you'd ever come back here, settle down with someone you love... and stay?"

The angry feeling that always shows up with such thoughts doesn't come, and I wonder why not. "That would be a thing, Jess. Now, wouldn't that be something?"

Yellow hair falls over Jessie's shoulders, and I know she doesn't want me to see the tears. "I'd like that. Going to bed now. You coming?"

"In a few minutes."

She stands, stretches, and lightly squeezes my shoulder. "I love you, Vi."

"Me too, you, Jess."

A little wind stirs up in Sinclair Woods and blows its way over here. It tickles the nape of my neck, and I shiver. A barn owl hoots, and fluttery wings lift into a starry sky. The words I said to Jessie echo in my heart. *That would be a thing, Jess. Now, wouldn't that be something?*

ACKNOWLEDGMENTS

WRITING THIS BOOK LED ME back through countless family paths, ones that were long hidden by time, and memory, and the process of living. A Celebration of Life Remembrance for my dear cousin, Jill Rosenthal, began this book's journey. The wise counsel of my son, Colin Stewart, and two other cousins, Tim Edgar and Karen Fischer, helped illuminate the way. Thanks to my parents, George and Helen Rosenthal, for childhood vacations to the Missouri Ozarks, most notably the Lake Taneycomo area, *Beulah Land*'s setting, where I spent happy days getting to know local folks, their customs, and their hearts.

A special debt of thanks goes to my Tampa Bay critique group—Corinne Gaile, Eileen Goldenberg, Joni Klein-Higger, Shannon Hitchcock, Debra Schlact, and Diana Sharp—without whose judicious and always spot-on advice, *Beulah Land* would be a shadow of a book. And to my online critique group—Beth Anderson, Susan Barker, and Jane Ellen Freeman—whose laser-like observations and analyses of every aspect of the manuscript were invaluable in moving the book ever forward to its conclusion.

A particular note of thanks to my husband Norman Stewart, who read and reread the manuscript from start to finish and whose suggestions were pivotal in the book's creation. Also, kudos to good friend, John Van Hoy, for being a beta reader and offering his insights on all things *Beulah Land*.

I am grateful for the wise leadership at Interlude Press and Duet, their Young Adult imprint, especially my editor, Annie Harper, whose guidance was invaluable beyond measure. And to Candysse Miller, Director of Marketing and Communications, and to C.B. Messer, Art Director, whose indefatigable energy and gifted eye, respectively, rounded out a triumphant team for any author.

Finally, to the brave people who have fought and continue to fight for basic human rights, this author salutes you. This book, for which I alone am responsible, is but a token of my admiration for your courage and perseverance and resolve. Safe home to you all.

ABOUT THE AUTHOR

Nancy Stewart has been a teacher of grade school children and a university professor of education, specializing in children's and young adult literature. She was fortunate to have lived in London for ten years with her husband and three sons. While there, she was a consultant to the University of Cambridge. But it was during her tenure as a professor that her love of words and stories and all those valuable life experiences aligned, and she began to write books for young people.

A frequent speaker and presenter at writing conferences throughout the United States, Nancy conducts workshops, seminars, and Skype visits for school children with a view to helping save our planet. A blogger with a worldwide audience, she focuses on all things pertaining to writing for kids. A member of the *Rate Your Story* team, she critiques books for prospective authors.

Nancy is the author of several bestselling books for young readers, including *One Pelican at a Time: A Story of the Gulf Oil Spill*, which received the Literary Classics Silver Award (2012), and *Sea Turtle Summer*, Literary Classics Gold Award winner (2012); both books received the Literary Classics Seal of Approval. The manuscript for her forthcoming young adult novel, *Beulah Land*

(Duet, November, 2017), received the State of Florida First Place Rising Kite Award from the Society of Children's Writers and Illustrators (SCBWI) in 2015.

CONNECT
WITH NANCY
ONLINE

🌐 nancystewartbooks.com
🐦 @stewartnancy
f nancy.rosenthalstewart
🅱 nancystewart.blogspot.com

For a reader's guide to **Beulah Land** and
book club prompts, please visit duetbooks.com.

an imprint of interlude **press**

 duetbooks.com
@DuetBooks
duetbooks
store.interludepress.com

also from **duet**

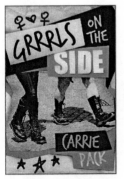

Grrrls on the Side by Carrie Pack

The year is 1994, and alternative is in, except for high schooler Tabitha Denton. Uninterested in boys, lonely, and sidelined by former friends, she finds her escape in a punk concert zine: an ad for a Riot Grrrl meet-up. There, Tabitha discovers herself, love, and how to stand up for what's right.

ISBN (print) 978-1-945053-21-4 | (eBook) 978-1-945053-37-5

The Seafarer's Kiss by Julia Ember

Mermaid Ersel rescues the maiden Ragna and learns the life she wants is above the sea. Desperate, Ersel makes a deal with Loki but the outcome is not what she expects. To fix her mistakes and be reunited with Ragna, Ersel must now outsmart the God of Lies.

ISBN (print) 978-1-945053-20-7 | (eBook) 978-1-945053-34-4

Not Your Sidekick by C.B. Lee

Welcome to Andover, where superpowers are common—but not for Jessica Tran. Despite her heroic lineage, Jess is resigned to a life without superpowers when an internship for Andover's resident super villain allows her to work alongside her longtime crush Abby and helps her unravel a plot larger than heroes and villains altogether.

ISBN (print) 978-1-945053-03-0 | (eBook) 978-1-945053-04-7